W9-AHB-034

"Entirely gripping and fast-paced."

—Lucy Christopher, award-winning author of *Stolen*

"A compelling story of terror, betrayal, and heroism... This brutal, emotionally charged novel will grip readers and leave them brokenhearted."

—*Kirkus Reviews*

"Love, loyalty, bravery, and loss meld into a chaotic, heart-wrenching mélange of issues that unite some and divide others. A highly diverse cast of characters, paired with vivid imagery and close attention to detail, set the stage for an engrossing, unrelenting tale."

—*Publishers Weekly*

"A gritty, emotional, and suspenseful read and although fictionalized, it reflects on a problematic and harrowing issue across the nation."

—BuzzFeed

"Marieke Nijkamp's brutal, powerful fictional account of a school shooting is important in its timeliness."

—Bustle.com

"A compelling, brutal story of an unfortunately all-too familiar situation: a school shooting. Nijkamp portrays the events thoughtfully, recounting fifty-four intense minutes of bravery, love, and loss."

—Book Riot

BEFORE I LET GO

ALSO BY MARIEKE NIJKAMP

This Is Where It Ends

before I
let go

MARIEKE NIJKAMP

Published by Sourcebooks Fire, an imprint of Sourcebooks, Inc.
P.O. Box 4410, Naperville, Illinois 60567-4410
(630) 961-3900
Fax: (630) 961-2168
www.sourcebooks.com

Library of Congress Cataloging-in-Publication data is on file with the
publisher.

Printed and bound in the United States of America.
BVG 10 9 8 7 6 5 4 3 2 1

To the ones we lost along the way

....

As the story goes, the town of Lost Creek, Alaska, isn't named after the eponymous stream. It's named after its first group of colonial settlers, a handful of adventurers for whom the world didn't have a place anymore. Lost men, who didn't belong anywhere else. They set down their roots, stealing land that was never theirs, and carved their home between the mountains and the mines, the hot springs, the river, and the lake, during those long summer days when anything seemed possible.

Then the cold came. And these settlers discovered that they had built their home in the heart of winter. They'd come for new opportunity, but they found that winter is not malleable, and frost settles too. And no matter how hard they tried, they could not escape being lost.

....

DAY ONE

MIDNIGHT FLIGHT

THE AIRPLANE'S ENGINES RUMBLE. THE SHADES ARE drawn, and the lights are on low. The few passengers around me listen to music or try to sleep in their uncomfortable seats as we fly toward a harsher winter.

I can't sleep. I haven't been able to since the call came. I stare blankly at the seat in front of me, but all I can see is her. Dark curls. Hazel eyes. Big heart. A girl who smiled even when the sun did not rise in the morning, who laughed in the face of darkness, who embraced her nights and cherished her days.

She took my heart and held it safe. She promised to

wait for me, with words that echo in my mind and tender touches I can still feel on my skin.

She.

Kyra.

Mine.

Let me tell you a story.

She was my best friend. She was my everything. And I lost her.

PHONE CALL

"Corey?"

"Mom? I just got back from the gym with Noa, and Eileen gave me your message. What's wrong? Are you okay? Is it Luke? What happened?"

"Luke's all right, honey. But I got a call this morning. I—I wanted you to hear it from me…"

"A call?"

"Lynda—Mrs. Henderson. Something happened in Lost Creek."

"Kyra? Did she have an episode? Did she run away again?"

"No, it's not that. It's… She…"

"Mom, tell me. Please."

"Corey, I'm sorry."

"Mom, are you crying?"

"No one knows quite what happened, but they think she wandered across the lake and found a weak spot. They found her under the ice."

"Wait—what?"

"She drowned. Kyra's d—"

"No."

"Corey…"

"No. No."

"Corey, sweetheart, listen to me."

"No. I don't want to hear this. I don't believe you."

"Corey—Corey. Slow breaths. Listen to me. I spoke to your headmistress. Come home."

"No."

"You're hurting—"

"Kyra can't be dead. She promised to wait for me. She knows I'm coming to visit. She can't be dead."

"Lynda thinks—"

"It's the first week of January! The lake should be frozen solid! It's not possible."

"Sheriff Flynn is investigating, but nothing suggests that her death was suspicious. Honey, Lynda thinks Kyra went looking for a crack in the ice."

"No, no, no."

"Kyra was ill. They tried to help her, but sometimes there's nothing anyone can do."

"I shouldn't have left her. I never even replied to her last letters."

"Oh, Corey."

"I need to go to Lost, Mom. I promised I'd go back to her. I promised."

"Come here first. Come home. I know I worked a lot of overtime at the hospital over the holidays, but come home. We'll postpone your trip and spend time together, just the three of us."

"I'd like that. I would, Mom. But I can't not go. Can I still stay with the Hendersons?"

"Yes, but—"

"I need to go home-home, Mom. I'm sorry."

"I never knew, between the two of you girls, who was more headstrong. Lynda said the school will host a memorial service next week. And Joe found a handwritten letter to you in her room. He thought having it might help. I'll forward you his email with the photo."

"Thanks."

"Honey, everyone will understand if you want to cancel your trip."

"I'll be there. I want to go. I need to go."

Kyra needs me.

LETTER FROM KYRA TO COREY
UNSENT

A bonfire lights the town square to mark the longest night. Remember how we thought that the world would be a happier place with more celebrations? I'm not sure that's true. I'm not sure I'm happier.

Someone left me salmonberries and flowers this morning. People do that a lot these days. Where the fruit and the flowers come from, I don't know. Jan's grocery store doesn't sell them. Yet here they are.

How is life outside the boundaries of endless time? Are you enjoying your classes at St. James? Are you as happy as I thought you would be?

I hope you are. I know you never wanted to

escape, but I'm glad you did. I can't wait to escape too. I'm trying so hard to wait for you. But it's hard, Cor. Lost is emptier now that you're gone. And I'm lonelier. I'm less without you, and Lost wants more. I don't remember the last time I slept. I don't remember the last time I smiled. The night is not dark enough. The stars you love still whisper their secrets, but sometimes I think I know too much. Around here, everyone wants answers, but I am the only one with questions.

I miss you.

I miss the dark nights.

I miss the dawn.

I miss you.

And I'm sorry.

—Kyra

A LAND OF GOLD AND LONELINESS

THE AIRPORT IS QUIET, STERILE. THIS EARLY IN THE morning, the few people in the terminal are lost in predawn slumber, and I am lost too. I've been traveling for thirteen hours. Three thousand miles. I settle on the floor in front of the tall glass windows as Alaska wakes up to another day with scarce sunlight. I watch planes taxi to and from the runways.

In the reflection of the window, a young girl stares at me. She sits a few seats down, her dress bright against the darkness outside and the gray of the terminal. Although she can't be more than eight or nine, even younger than my brother, I don't see anyone with her. The traveler to her left rests his head against his backpack, but he keeps shifting, as if in a restless sleep. An elderly couple reads a day-old newspaper. And the girl's eyes meet mine.

She holds a handful of flowers in front of her green dress. The petals are a familiar magenta, and she picks them off one at a time.

Salmonberries don't grow here, not at an airport on the outskirts of a city. They're not the kind of flower you'd find at a florist's shop, and they certainly don't bloom in January. The girl holds flowers that shouldn't be. From this distance, I shouldn't be able to hear what she's saying either, but I do, as clearly as if she were standing next to me.

Endless day, endless night, come to set your heart alight.

With each cadence, she plucks off another petal.

At the end of her tune, she smiles.

My heart stutters. I clamber to my feet and turn to get a better look at her. But the waiting area is nearly empty. I spot the backpacker. The elderly couple. A family with twin boys. There's no sign of the girl, as if she'd only existed in the window's reflection.

Except that flower petals lie scattered across the floor, and her voice still swirls around me, singing the song that Kyra sang to me first.

Endless night, endless day, come to steal your soul away.

....

The fifth and final leg of the trip gets me going. I cling to my coffee, the deception of daylight, and a combination of restlessness and homesickness. I transfer to a small floatplane that will fly me northwest, to Lost Creek, where I'll stay for the next five days, until another plane can bring me back here. Cramming my backpack into the seat next to me, I buckle up behind the pilot. I nod to him, but from the moment we take off, my forehead is glued to the window.

The lights of Fairbanks International Airport glimmer below us. To the east, the city glows electric and yellow under a blanket of clouds. At the start of the year, Fairbanks sees fewer than four hours of sunlight a day, and Lost Creek fewer still.

Kyra loved coming to Fairbanks. She thought Lost was claustrophobic. She wanted to travel. She wanted to study and explore. But the city never called to me. It always felt too large, too anonymous. Life may be softer here, the winters less threatening, but back home in Lost, people looked out for one another. In our tight-knit community, surrounded by nothing for miles, we had each other and the deep blue of twilight. To me, Lost felt safe.

Even now, I'm more at ease at St. James's small boarding school in Dauphin than I am in the large house Mom bought in Winnipeg. She calls the neighborhood affluent and prosperous, though people never leave the confines of their own yards. Mom is rarely there to notice because she works long days at the children's hospital. At least at school I have a community, friends, teammates. Still, we may have made our home in Canada, but I left my heart in Lost.

The plane leans north, and Fairbanks disappears behind us. We fly to an otherworldly place, one that does not play by the same rules. The evergreens wear an armor of snow. The air shimmers with cold. Lost Creek is godforsaken, with winters that feel cruel and permanent, and we are proud of our resilience. The journey to Lost is a rush of turbulence through snow and memories, and the refrain of those same awful words: *Endless night, endless day. Come to steal your soul away.*

By the time Lost comes into view, I'm spread thin by exhaustion and fear. Time flies like we do, and I'm not ready. I'm not ready to face that Kyra won't be waiting for me, and I'm not sure I ever will be. I'm torn between homesickness so deep it aches and the debilitating uncertainty of what lies ahead, of not understanding what happened to my best friend.

I push my nails deep into the palms of my hands and keep my eyes on the landscape as we prepare to land. To the left are the camping grounds where a handful of tourists spend their summers fishing on the lake and hunting bears in the woods. The cabins are abandoned in winter, groaning under their blanket of snow.

To the right are the old mining works. Gold is still rumored to lie beneath the hills—or heavy metals, perhaps—but the easily accessible ores were all exhausted decades ago. Mining deeper would be expensive, and our mine is too small to be profitable. What lies under the land may hold promises of riches, but for Lost Creek, those promises are empty, and people know better than to rush now. Our community has grown to depend on itself and the carefully cultivated land, not on the unpredictable nature.

Our community. Lost Creek, established in 1898, population 247.

I breathe. *Two hundred forty-six.*

Bordered by its eponymous river, Lost Creek stands against the elements. Our small, narrow, gold-rush town has a police station, a combined elementary and high school, an office for the doctor with whom Mom often worked, a moderately well-stocked grocery store, a bakery, a sole café/pub, a post office/tourist center, and an abandoned spa with hot springs, which sits outside the borders of town. The spa is a dash of color on the bleak horizon. The first time Kyra and I went there, we thought it was a superhero headquarters.

The landing gear hits the ground with a jolt and my seat belt strains against my lap from the force. We bump to a stop. This runway and the single road through the interior are the only paths that connect Lost Creek to civilization.

These two connections to the outside world used to be all we needed to survive. Nothing could harm us within these borders. Within this community, we stood together. All of Lost against the rest of the world.

All of us.

All of us except one. All of us except Kyra, who never felt like she belonged. She never cared for hunting or camping. Like her grandfather, Kyra wanted to study storytelling. She collected the town's myths and legends, and she was always curious about what lay beyond. But Lost is a town that thrives on secrets, and in Kyra, all of Lost's secrets lay exposed.

STARS AND STORIES

TWO YEARS BEFORE

IN LOST, THE EASIEST WAY TO FIT IN IS TO FALL INTO THE town's rhythm. And on the days when Kyra wasn't with me, I did. I did my homework and my chores. I didn't talk back to the adults in town. I kept an eye on Luke when Mom was away. I had my stars in the sky, and I didn't need to go anywhere to observe them.

"It should be enough," I told Kyra, when I snuck into her room at midnight.

She sat at her desk, a blanket wrapped around her shoulders, half a dozen books open in front of her. Her knees were pulled up to her chin, glasses perched on the tip of her nose. She'd been waiting for me. Of course she had. It was exactly three years since Dad left and—aside from calls and cards on birthdays—was never heard from again. I hated that anniversary. I didn't want to be alone.

Kyra closed her books, one by one. "What should be enough?"

"All of this. I have you and Luke and Mom. Astronomy and home. I don't want to be as restless as I am. I don't want to care about him anymore. All of this should be enough."

"Why?"

I shrugged.

She sat down on her bed and invited me under the blanket. "You're allowed to be angry. You can be hurt. And more than that, I don't think you should ever settle for 'enough.' Enough by whose standards, anyway?"

I leaned into her. My hands were cold from the night air, but she didn't flinch. She pulled the blanket up higher.

"Mine, I guess?" I said. "Or Lost's?"

"Hopefully those aren't the same," she teased. "What do you dream about?" And then, after a beat, "What would you dream about if it weren't for Lost?"

Because she was right. Those weren't the same. If not for Lost, I would go off to college to study astronomy. Work at one of the observatories around Fairbanks. Maybe study the aurora borealis.

But having Kyra next to me made me feel even braver. "Work on the Giant Magellan Telescope in Chile, to study the evolution of galaxies," I answered. Once it was completed, the GMT would be the largest optical observatory in the world, ten times stronger than the Hubble Space Telescope. "Or on the E-ELT, to study the evolution of dark matter in high redshift galaxies."

I stole a sideways glance at Kyra, who blinked at me owlishly. "I didn't even understand those words separately, let alone together."

I giggled and it bubbled into laughter. I didn't know how Kyra did it, but she focused my restlessness like a telescope, away from the dark energy of Dad's absence and toward the exoplanets of possibility.

"I'll come to visit you in Chile," Kyra said. "And then I'll drag you with me to Antarctica. We'll see what the other side of the world looks like. See the southern lights together. I'll tell you stories about them." A smile tugged at her lips. "What if they're upside down?"

I scowled. "That's not how science works."

She grinned.

I punched her softly in the arm. "What will you do until then?"

"Travel too, if I can. Study narrative culture around the Arctic." She motioned to one of the books on her desk. "I don't want to collect and claim stories like Granddad did.

I want to be respectful to Indigenous cultures. But I want to understand how our stories came to be. I don't want them, and our histories, to melt along with the ice."

"Do you think you'll be able to?" I asked, wondering, *Will Kyra get out of here? Pursue her dreams? Be well enough to do so?*

She recoiled, as if I'd hit her. "Yes. Somehow or other, I'll find a way."

"Then we'll have to find a good college for both of us," I offered.

Kyra rested her head back on the pillow. "We'll go farther than anyone in Lost ever has. Adventurers, looking for stories and stars."

"But we'll always come home, right?" I asked.

She looked up at me. "Maybe. Maybe I'll get lost on the ice instead."

UNPREDICTABLE

A YEAR AND A HALF BEFORE

Kyra didn't keep her head down. She didn't fit in.

She's crazy. The words followed her wherever she went. In the conservative, white world of Lost, standing out was a mortal sin. When she came to school, the other juniors and seniors in our class would slide their desks away from us. They'd invite me over for hot chocolate after class, but never her. They'd steal her books. They'd throw her homework—and sometimes the essays she wrote on storytelling—into White Wolf Lake.

She kept her head held high. She never let me yell at

them. And she never let anyone but me see how much their cruelty hurt her.

She's crazy. Batshit. Insane. Nuts. A freak.

The people of Lost Creek had a particular affinity for that last word. *Freak*. It floated around her, spoken in hatred and whispered in fear.

And fear was the worst part. Too often, people who'd known her since she was a baby, who'd watched her grow up, would talk about her as if she were a threat. And they weren't even subtle about it.

They wanted her gone.

"Joe, I've heard about a good residential treatment center in Fairbanks. It might be better for your daughter there," Mr. Lucas would say.

"We've been over this a million times. No," Mr. Henderson would reply.

"You have to understand it from my point of view. Kyra goes to the same school as my daughters."

"And she has since they were all toddlers."

"But now she has this *diagnosis*. What if something happens? What if—"

"What could possibly happen?"

"What if she sna—what if she has one of her episodes?"

"When she has one of her episodes, she *paints*. Do you think your daughters are in danger from Kyra's crafts?"

But that, of course, wasn't Mr. Lucas's point. It

was never anyone's point. They weren't worried about the creative ways Kyra burned off energy; they were worried about her escapades. When her manic episodes overwhelmed her, she became unstoppable. She could lose herself in the woods for days. Once, she snuck to the river and dumped the fishermen's catch back into the water. Another time, she ventured down the closed mine, and it took our parents the better part of a day and a night to find her.

The people of Lost were worried because they had seen her vanish. They were convinced that she'd drag one of them along, and that they'd stray too far. That they, too, would disappear in the dangerous terrain outside of Lost. But she wouldn't do that. Kyra pushed everyone away during those episodes. Even me.

So Mr. H would willfully misunderstand the community's remarks. Eventually, out of respect for him and his status as the owner of the mine, they'd concede that, of course, they were only worried about Kyra's welfare.

But every time she overheard one of those conversations, Kyra would stare at me with tears in her eyes. The first time it happened, I tried to explain the town's fear, but she challenged it. We were sitting in her window seat, and she tensed all over, her cheeks turning pink with frustration. The second time, she ran away.

I'd lost count of the incidents since then, but this time,

she was still in flight mode when she asked me, "I'm not enough, am I?"

"You should never settle for 'enough.'" I hoped that hearing the same words she'd told me would make her feel braver.

"You know, a couple of centuries ago, I would've been called a witch." She clung to her windowsill, as if to stop herself from running away from all of us, and all of this. "They would've burned me at the stake."

"I wouldn't have let them."

"Do you think I should go? To the treatment center in Fairbanks?"

"Only if you want to. Only if you think it'll help. But not because the rest of the town has forgotten who you really are. If that's the only reason, I'd rather you stay here with me."

"I want to feel better. I want to get these episodes under control." Her shoulders drooped. "I want to belong here, like you and Luke do."

I stared at her for the longest time. The setting sun cast her face in an orange glow, making her hair look auburn and her hazel eyes almost green. I loved Lost, because it was the only home I'd ever known, but I hated how the town had treated her since she was diagnosed with bipolar disorder a year before. It was as if, overnight, they'd decided that she was no longer the girl they knew, but a danger. "I want you to feel better. I want you to belong too."

"Why is everyone so afraid of me?"

"Because you're unpredictable." *Like spring storms and inaccessible mines.* "In Lost, unpredictability has never been good."

STRANGERS, TRAITORS, GHOSTS

I OPEN THE DOOR AND JUMP OUT OF THE PLANE AS SOON as we land on the narrow strip. The concrete shocks my knees and I stretch in the freezing cold air. I expect to find Mr. Henderson's 4x4 waiting for me, or Sheriff Flynn, maybe. Instead, a lone figure stands against the rising sun. With the light at her back, I can only see her silhouette—a tall, gangly figure whose long hair dances in the wind. She raises a hesitant hand.

My heart skips a beat. *Kyra*. Without thinking, I start toward her, her name on the tip of my tongue.

Then the light clears. Her nose is smaller. Her hair lighter.

And the shout of recognition dies in my throat.

Piper Morden.

Not Kyra.

I forgot. Now I ache to forget again.

Behind me, the pilot disembarks. He grabs my backpack and hands it to me. "Your return flight is booked. Be here on time. See you in five days."

So little time, but it has to be enough. "I'll make sure of it. Thank you."

The man hesitates, then says, "Be careful in Lost Creek. Not everything is as it seems here."

Before I can reply with a simple, *I know. We've always gone our own way*, he turns on his heels with military precision and stalks back to the plane. I head toward Piper, who smirks. Plenty of people don't understand our closed community, our way of living. We're all used to odd comments like these.

Piper wraps her arms around me. She's never done so before, but I cling to her. She's strong and familiar. She smells of winter and home. "Hey, big city girl."

"Hey."

"How was your flight?"

"It was good. Quiet. Early." *Strange*.

"I can only imagine." Her smile fades. "Mr. H has a business meeting, so he asked me to pick you up. We're glad you're here. Kyra would've liked that."

That's new. These last few years, Piper never

considered Kyra's feelings, and now that she's dead doesn't seem like the right time to start.

I sling my backpack over my shoulders, wondering how to phrase this question without sounding accusatory. "What can I expect here, Piper? I know Kyra wasn't exactly…loved."

Piper stiffens as if I'd slapped her. Then she flicks a wayward lock of hair out of her face. "Do you think us so cold that we wouldn't mourn her?"

"No, but—"

"Things changed after you left."

"Nothing ever changes in Lost Creek," I say, out of habit. The only way to mark the passage of time here is by the aging of the children. They grow older, as they're meant to, every birthday the start of a new year. The adults somehow appear to stop aging, and the elderly stop counting the years altogether.

Piper's mouth quirks up, twisting her face into a harsh grimace. "Never mind. You'll come to understand."

"Understand what?" I ask, but Piper has already turned away from me.

"We take care of our own here. You ought to know that."

I trek after her and regret not changing into my bunny boots. My sneakers are fit for traveling, but not for withstanding miles of snow. The cold bites.

At least I've arrived with the sun. When Piper and

I turn away from the airstrip, toward Lost, bright light peeks out over the horizon. Anticipation takes over and the churning in my stomach settles. I breathe. This is home. The zingy smell of ice in the air. The snow, layered over the permafrost, that crunches beneath our feet.

Amid the gentle hills and pine tree forests lies the town of Lost Creek. Our small, private universe. From our vantage point, it looks tiny, like a collection of dollhouses rather than a place where people live.

But it is home.

Welcome home.

Piper leads me as if I didn't know my way around. We walk along the single road toward Main Street, one of a grand total of five streets in Lost Creek. It's also the town's busiest street.

On any given day of the week, Main would be crowded. Even in the middle of winter, this is where the gossip gets shared and the grocery store and the physician's pharmacy are stocked, where fishermen return from their camps along the creek with their catch.

But today is different.

The grocery store is closed. The street is abandoned. Well-kept houses are the only assurance that people actually live here. Fresh paint makes the town look newer than I've ever seen it. When I left, the houses were weatherworn and lived-through, perennially smudged with sleet and mud. Today, they are pristine. A dash of color sidles up the wall of the old post office, though from this angle, I can't make out the design. It's as if, with Kyra gone, Lost had painted over all its cracks and creases.

"What happened here?" I ask.

"Hope," Piper says quietly. She reverently touches a ribbon tied around a gate. "And remembrance."

I raise my eyebrows. "What does that mean?"

Piper doesn't answer, but now I notice the ribbons are everywhere, tied around every flagpole and every door handle. Bows in magenta and black—Kyra's favorite color and the color of mourning. It's like Lost is demonstrating its sorrow. But we've never made our grief public, beyond memorial gatherings. When Kyra's grandfather passed away, the town honored him with a somber service. And *he* was liked by everyone.

It must be a coincidence.

"Look, I'm sorry if you thought I was being harsh before," I try. "I just want to understand what happened to Kyra."

Piper shakes her head. Her gaze searches Main. I have no idea what she's looking for, but I glance surreptitiously over my own shoulder. We're as alone as we were the moment we stepped into town. The street is empty, and the sunlight isn't as bright here. The shadows are longer and darker.

"You'll find out," Piper says. "Someday, you'll understand."

The wind picks up, weaving around the houses and whispering.

Stranger.

Traitor.

Outsider.

The words float in the same tune as the girl's at the airport, soft and out of reach. I swirl around, but no one's there.

I pull at the straps of my backpack to cinch it closer and fall into step with Piper, who keeps a firm pace. She doesn't seem to mind the wind. Or maybe she doesn't hear it.

At the turn that leads to my old house, I pause. Piper grabs my hand and pulls me in the other direction.

"I promised Mrs. Henderson I would take you to her as soon as you arrived, but once you've settled in, you should walk over." Her voice is neutral.

We follow a side street until we reach a large, nineteenth-century town house on the edge of the creek. It's the biggest plot of land in Lost, barring the spa outside the town's borders. When settlers arrived in Lost Creek, Mr. Henderson's great-grandfather was the first to find gold here—and his grandfather, the last. Over the years, the Henderson family had built a legacy of industry and investment. And although Mr. Henderson hasn't been able to reopen our mine, it's only right that their house reflects their status.

But while the house may appear imposing to outsiders, to Kyra and me, it was home. And now it's in mourning. I drop my backpack and gape.

The gate and flagpole are covered with black ribbons. On either side of the driveway, small flowers lie strewn across the snow. Bright pink salmonberry flowers. They're the same flowers the girl at the airport held. They're the same flowers Kyra used to scatter around town.

I squint. No, not blossoms, but flowers made of magenta ribbons, like the ones that hang on Main Street. They remind me of Kyra's paintings from her manic periods—not quite real enough, but still too close for comfort.

Maybe, just maybe, life is still a little unpredictable here.

"He was right, you know." Piper's words are so soft, they don't immediately register.

"Who?" I ask.

"The pilot. Not everything is as it seems. I'll see you at the service, if I don't see you before then. Come find me if you have questions." She starts back toward Main.

"Piper?"

She pauses and turns. "Yes?"

My stomach roils. *Wait. Don't leave me. I can't face Kyra's absence yet. Let me cling for one more moment to the world I used to know.*

I hesitate. "Tell Tobias that Luke said hi?"

At this, Piper smiles again, but I know it's not for me. "Of course."

Although Piper and I were friendly, we were never as close as our brothers. When Mom spent long days in Fairbanks and the surrounding towns seeing patients, I would often stay with Kyra, and Luke with Tobias. Luke had been furious when he found out that I'd made plans to come back to Lost to see Kyra without him. To see Kyra.

Before.

She knew I was coming. How could she not wait for me?

NOTE FROM KYRA TO COREY
SENT, UNANSWERED

    Can you see the stars at your new school? I can't imagine that the night sky there is as clear as it is in Lost. When you're back, let's go camping near the springs. Just you and me and a campfire and the northern lights. We'll build a bridge. A bridge between us. I miss you, Corey.

FRAMED MOMENTS

I PUSH OPEN THE GATE, WHICH SQUEAKS AGAINST THE cold, and hesitate.

The steps leading up to the Hendersons' front door are the same steps where Kyra used to wait for Mr. H when he came home from his business trips. Where she would wait for me those rare times when Mom, Luke, and I would go visit my uncle in Nome. She would sit on a stair, with a book or a notepad, which she'd drop as soon as she saw us, racing to meet us at the gate.

I want Kyra to run out to greet me, to tackle-hug me. But she doesn't. She isn't…

I am at Kyra's house, and Kyra's not here. I am home,

and Kyra's not. The weight of grief crashes over me like an avalanche.

The Hendersons' door opens. Mrs. Henderson steps onto the porch and folds her hands in front of her. Her black dress makes her face gaunt. A bewildered look haunts her eyes.

I launch myself at her, and she pulls me close. When she disentangles, she puts her hands on my arms and peers up at me. "Look at you, you've grown taller. We *missed* you. Joe is at a business meeting, but he'll be along shortly. Come, it's cold today and you must be hungry."

She steps aside to let me in. "You can stay in the guest room, if you want. Kyra's room is still there too, of course, but it's locked. We'd rather no one disturb it."

"I understand," I say. "Thank you for having me."

Mrs. Henderson keeps talking. Kyra used to ramble whenever she was upset too. "If you'd prefer to stay somewhere else, I'm sure we can arrange that. The Mordens have a spare bedroom. And Mrs. Robinson would accommodate you too, I'm sure."

"Don't worry, Mrs. H. I'm fine."

It's a lie. I'm not fine. I want to turn and run, but I stand in the foyer. The house is silent. It feels wrong. I drop my bag near the coatrack and shrug off my coat. Mrs. H is already heading toward the living room, but I linger in the hallway.

The Hendersons never had pictures on their walls, and growing up surrounded by Mom's photo albums, that was always odd to me. But now, pictures of Kyra hang everywhere. I wrap my arms around my waist and take in each one. Pictures of her as a small girl, of her growing up. Pictures of her drawing with charcoal, swimming in the hot springs, running around in costume. I remember each of those days.

I remember them. I was there. I was *here*.

But I'm not in any of the photos. They're all of Kyra. One frame draws my attention. A young Kyra in oversize fishing gear. It was the spring we both turned ten, and school had given us a work-experience assignment. We had to shadow someone at their day job, and Kyra decided we'd go fishing. We borrowed gear from the tourist center and joined Piper's father along the lakeshore. Five minutes in, Kyra decided that she hated sitting around waiting for fish to bite, but I loved it, so she stuck around. She caught a fish big enough for a meal and then some, and she was so proud that she posed with her catch. This isn't that photo, though. This is the one where we were sitting side by side, arms around each other's shoulders.

Except, I'm nowhere to be seen. Kyra is smiling alone.

Did Mrs. Henderson edit this? Do I just not remember this photo?

I take a step closer and reach for the frame when someone tuts. I turn toward the sound, but the hall is empty.

I back into the living room, but that has changed in a thousand small ways too. There's a new couch. A lamp has been moved to a table on the other side of the room. But most glaring are the half-dozen bouquets of wildflowers with condolence cards. Kyra abhorred grief. When her grandfather died, she walked out of the service, and she talked me into doing the same. She didn't want to mourn him; she wanted to celebrate him. But Lost didn't share that sentiment. They wanted their traditional, somber service.

Mrs. Henderson carries in a plate of her specialty sourdough muffins from the kitchen. They smell of sugar and comfort, potent reminders of all the times Kyra and I snuck freshly baked cookies and tablespoons of icing. My hands tingle as I remember the playful swat of Mrs. Henderson's spatula across our knuckles when she tried to scare us away. Suddenly my eyes burn, and I can't swallow back a sob.

Mrs. H sets the plate on the coffee table and pulls me into another hug. "Oh, *Corey*."

"I'm so sorry, Mrs. H," I whisper. "I wish I had come sooner." I can't articulate what I really want to say. That I left Kyra. That I should've paid more attention to her letters. That because of my absence and silence, her death is partially my fault. "I should have been here for her."

"It wasn't your choice, sweetheart," Mrs. H says as we sit down on the couch. "I'm sure Kyra understood. She was happy, you know. Near the end."

"How could she have possibly been happy?" That's something you say about someone old who has died, someone who lived a century. Not about a seventeen-year-old girl whose body was found floating under the ice after she cut her own life short. *She didn't* sound *happy*.

Mrs. Henderson gives a fragile smile. "She came home to us. I wish you could've seen how much she'd changed these last few months. She found her place here."

I blink. "She did?" *She never wrote about that to me. She still seemed to be struggling. Did I misunderstand? How much did she leave out?* "Oh. So they helped her in Fairbanks?"

"Oh no, she never went. We decided it would be better for her here."

Rowanne, Kyra's therapist, traveled between patients in various towns, just like Mom did as a physiotherapist. "But I thought Rowanne recom—"

"Rowanne stopped coming to Lost Creek shortly after your family left," Mrs. Henderson snaps. Her mouth thins and her eyes flash. I scoot back a little on the couch. "She abandoned Kyra."

I wince. "Then what changed? Did you find her another therapist? Better medication?"

Mrs. H looks at me as if I've grown two heads or started speaking in tongues. "Corey, after you left, Kyra finally understood that the community loved her too, that she *belonged* here. That was what made her happy. You can see it in her recent paintings, in her art. Lost gave her purpose. It set her heart and mind alight."

Alight. A shiver runs down my spine when I hear that word again.

"Lost Creek never accepted her like that."

Like Piper, Mrs. H's smile slips and she withdraws. "The town embraced her."

This was what Kyra wanted—to be accepted. "I didn't think she'd find that in Lost," I say very carefully.

"Well, she did, Corey. You weren't here."

I pick up one of the cups of tea Mrs. H set out for us. I let it warm my hands before I ask, "Then why did she leave? If she was so happy, why didn't she wait for me? She knew I was coming."

"No star can burn forever, Corey. You've always had a head for science, you must know that. It was Kyra's time to let go," she says, with almost religious reverence. Then she nods behind me. "It's beautiful, isn't it?"

I shift to see a painting resting on the floor behind the couch. The canvas is surrounded by bouquets, candles, and ribbons. Blood roars in my ears. The teacup tumbles from my hands.

I recognize it as one of Kyra's. The painting is so detailed, it's like looking at a photograph. A circle of blossoms is spread out over snow and ice. The flowers look so real it's as if they've been placed on top of the canvas itself.

The constellation of Orion reflects in the surface. The brightest red star—Betelgeuse—shines like the supernova it's turning into, and it lights up the painting. It lights up the ice.

It lights up the body beneath it.

Kyra had painted herself floating under the translucent ice. Her brown hair is spread out around her, and her hazel eyes are opened wide. Even as she sinks into the dark abyss of the lake, she smiles.

And I'm numb.

LOSS

MRS. H HELPS ME CLEAN UP MY SPILLED TEA WITH A forced smile. She won't comment on the painting, beyond the quality of the art, and I can't find the words to ask her when Kyra made this canvas—how long she knew this was coming, and why the Hendersons didn't think to question their daughter about her painting. It makes no sense. How can Mrs. Henderson stare at this image wistfully, talking about color and shadow, when I want to cover it up and never see it again?

Instead, I focus on Mrs. H. The timbre of her voice used to soothe me. Kyra and I would spend hours at her house or in her bakery, listening to her gossip while she worked. But now, her voice chafes. I don't want to hear about how this year's catch is terrible, or how the Halwoods' marriage ended with Anna hitching a ride out of town in the mail plane, or even about the potential opportunities for Mr. H's mine and the buzz of hope that brings to the mining families in town. I just want to know what happened to my best friend.

Her chatter is interrupted when Mr. H walks in with company. Kyra was lanky like her father and shared his intelligent eyes, but now Mr. H has grown pale and gray. He pulls me into a hug. The smell of his cologne is so familiar, I feel like I never left.

"I'm so sorry, Mr. H." My voice catches. "I wish I could have been here."

"Corey. Kyra would've appreciated you being here now," he says.

"What happened?" I blurt out.

"I lost my daughter," Mr. H says. He exhales. "It was her time."

His words are spoken with so much pain, such finality, that I know there's no reopening the conversation, despite all the questions I carry with me. The only soft words that Mr. H ever had were for Kyra. I wonder what he'll do with them now.

I turn to the middle-aged, brown-skinned man standing behind Mr. H. He's wearing a fancy suit that makes him looks like he got sidetracked on his way to one of the cities. Mr. H's associates rarely make it out to Lost. But I guess if Mr. H can't leave to do business, his business comes to him.

"You must be young Kyra's friend," the man says. His words are measured, careful but pleasant. "My name is Mr. Sarin."

"Corey. Corey Johnson."

"I'm sorry for the loss of your friend, Ms. Johnson. It is a tragedy to lose one so young, especially a girl who was liked and respected by all."

The Lost Creek I knew never respected Kyra. They didn't care about her art, and they didn't care about her. But I don't tell him that. Raw emotions make the memories too harsh, make the truth hurt too much. "She deserved so much more."

"Death is a thief," Mr. Sarin says after a moment. His expression is filled with kind concern. "It slips into our lives and steals what we care about most. It breaks us, and even when we piece ourselves together again, the pain remains. My son knows that feeling and so do I, but..." He hesitates. "I believe that even death is not beyond hope. Kyra cared deeply for you. Perhaps you will believe that she still watches out for Lost Creek. Perhaps you'll believe that she still watches out for you."

"She is," I whisper. Because I'm here now, I kept my

promise to return to Lost, to her. And despite everything that has changed, part of me believes that somewhere, somehow, Kyra is still waiting for me.

SAINTS AND SOURDOUGH

A YEAR AND A HALF BEFORE

IF IT WERE UP TO LOST, THEY WOULD HAVE FORGOTTEN that Kyra existed. Long gone were the memories of the young girl they used to know, before she started showing symptoms in her early teens. The girl who laughed at the right jokes and behaved appropriately, as they expected. Not the girl who wandered through town for nights on end and threatened their way of being by sharing their secrets with an outsider—even if that outsider was her therapist.

And when Kyra's highs dimmed and she fell into

darkness, when she locked herself in her room and slept through the long nights, Lost went about its days as if nothing were wrong. The only difference was that those were the days when I belonged again because I wasn't marred by her presence. Those were the days I had other friends too.

I never told Kyra that, and she never asked.

It was a particularly cold spring day, after the ice broke up, when the entire school congregated in Claja, the small pub at the edge of Lost. Restless energy buzzed around me. By night, this pub was the gathering place for Lost's fishermen and workers. By day, it doubled as a café for high school students. It was where everyone went after school was out and before our parents needed us. We would gather and gossip and play games and drink hot chocolate.

I wasn't supposed to be there. Kyra and I had planned to hole up in the old spa to do our homework. But she went home before school ended and when I swung by her house, she didn't want to see me—or anyone. So I was left with what Lost considered a "normal" weekday afternoon.

The only open seat was at a table with Piper and Sam Flynn, the sheriff's son. They'd both always been kind to me, in school and out. They beckoned me over.

Neither of them had spoken a word *to* Kyra since her diagnosis, as far as I could tell. It was amazing how you could be invisible in Lost Creek, even if you didn't want to be. But I knew from experience that everyone loved to talk *about* Kyra. Treatment options. Scary stories about people who "snapped" and became violent. Some speculated about whether she was lying to get attention, not that it would make her any more popular.

Piper usually kept her cool, but that day, she too declared Kyra an outsider.

"Don't be ridiculous," I spat at her. "Her family's been part of Lost Creek for generations. She's lived here all her life. She's no outsider."

Piper shrugged. "Maybe not by blood, but you can't deny that she's a freak. She's not one of us."

"She always has been," I shot back. Heat flushed through me.

"Not anymore."

Not anymore. Not since Kyra first started having episodes. Not since the diagnosis. I didn't think two simple words could have such an impact. I shook my head. "No. She's still the same Kyra, and if you can't accept that, it says a whole lot more about you than it does about her."

I would've moved to another table, but there was nowhere else to go. After a long silence, Piper pushed a plate with chocolate chip cookies from Mrs. H's bakery toward me. "I'm sorry. I really am. I know it must be difficult being her friend."

I'd heard that before. A thousand times, and a thousand times too many.

On the other side of the table, Sam winced and looked away. He rarely spoke and he never smiled, but he was never purposely cruel either.

Anger boiled within me, churning through my body, from my stomach to my fingertips. I was tired. Of their assumptions. Of having to defend our friendship. I looked out the window. The snow distorted the people outside, bundled up in their warmest clothes. "It's no harder to be Kyra's friend than it is to be yours or anyone else's."

"I think you're a saint for putting up with her," she said. She smiled and nudged the plate a little farther. She didn't want me to be offended. And I was a coward, not telling her how much her words hurt. Instead, I accepted a cookie, as a peace offering, and told her what I knew to be true.

"She's one of us, Piper. We've lived through the same winters. She's one of us. And she always will be."

DOORWAYS

MR. H AND MR. SARIN BOTH STAY FOR A CUP OF TEA AND a sourdough muffin. Afterward, Mr. H leads me to the outbuilding that stands a little ways from the main house. The cabin is almost as old as the house itself. It's had a lot of purposes over the years. Originally, it was used for wood storage and after that, I think, as a garage. When Kyra's grandfather couldn't live in his small apartment on Main on his own anymore, Mr. H had the outbuilding completely refurbished into a small, two-room residential space with a kitchenette and bathroom. Kyra's grandfather lived there for the last years of his life, and after that, Kyra claimed it. She wanted a larger room for her books, magazines, comics, and notebooks, and studio space to paint whenever her manic episodes left her restless and eager to create. It became a hideout for the two of us.

More than anywhere else, this was our home.

As Mr. H unlocks the door, I notice more salmonberry flowers on the windowsill. Kyra mentioned these flowers in her last letter, but that seems to be the only detail that fits with what she wrote about the town and what everyone here is saying.

Inside, I set down my bag in the room that used to be Kyra's studio and her grandfather's library before that. Now, it's as sterile and uncomfortable as a new school uniform. Kyra's paints and crafts have been removed, and the room has been stripped. Only the old desk and a guest bed remain.

But Kyra's bedroom door is exactly the way I remember it: painted in bright colors with superheroes sketched all over it. The design changed often, depending on what series she liked best. Last summer, the night before we moved, she painted over a sketch of the Young Avengers and added the Congress of Worlds. Thor stands front and center, and her eyes follow me.

I cross the room and trace the lines on the door. I used to tease Kyra about her fascination with comics, but she took it in stride.

"People have used art and graphics to tell stories for

centuries," she said once. "We could all do with more heroes and tricksters and storytellers."

I told her, "I'd rather have stars than heroes."

She laughed. "That's why we have constellations. To preserve our stories and our heroes in the stars."

Now I'll never hear her laugh again. And it hurts. It *hurts*.

"We're keeping the door locked," Mr. H says. "At least until we decide what to do with Kyra's room."

With that, he leaves me. I'm glad to be alone and don't want to be alone at the same time. A chill passes over me.

I take a shower in the tiny bathroom to warm up and wash the travel off of me. Under the hot water, I try to rub away the dark shadows under my eyes, to no avail. Grief cloaks me like a shroud.

As I'm pulling on a turtleneck sweater, a floorboard creaks in Kyra's room, and I sob-laugh at the moods of this old house.

Kyra's bedroom was mine as much as it was hers. Even though my family used to live a few blocks away, even though this little cabin squeaked and groaned around us, Kyra hosted all of our sleepovers. We had everything here. A place for our adventures. An easy route to sneak out. Privacy. Freedom.

It shouldn't be a tomb.

But as long as Kyra's door remains locked, all of our memories in this place are protected. As long as Kyra's door remains locked, I can convince myself it's just another winter morning in Lost Creek, when I rose before twilight and Kyra slept until noon. And I can sit here and stare at the door, waiting for her to wake.

Perhaps that's true for Mr. and Mrs. H too. As long as the door remains locked, the room on the other side can hold *anything*.

I shake my head and reach for my coat. Kyra would tell me to get up, get out, go do something. Go into town and bring back stories. She'd tell me to remember her instead of mourn her.

After a moment of indecision, I stuff my phone into my pocket. Reception in Lost is spotty at best, but I've picked up some bad habits from the world outside.

I inch open the door and pause before stepping out. A faint humming filters in. Kyra's song. The whispers come again, so soft I'm not sure if I truly hear them or if they're my own subconscious scolding me.

Deserter.

You abandoned her.

You never knew her.

Stranger.

Traitor.

You were never her friend.

Then silence.

I convince myself it's all in my head.

THE LONELY LAKE

I SWING BY THE MAIN HOUSE TO HAND MY PASSPORT TO Mrs. H for safekeeping. It's habit more than necessity. Lost has little crime, but I don't like leaving it lying around. She takes it, then shoos me away. She's baking. Grief baking, she calls it, and I would only get underfoot.

I could go into town to see if Sam is around, or Tobias maybe. I could talk to Mrs. Morden at the post office, trade Kyra stories with her. But my feet take me along the narrow path leading to the outskirts of town. I keep walking until, just south of Lost, I reach the creek that leads to White Wolf Lake.

I push the hem of my pants into my boots and begin to

run. The rhythm of my steps calms me. Kyra and I raced along the creek so many times I lost track.

The wind plays with the soft snow, blowing gusts of white across the ice. The pine trees on either side of the deep, dark lake spread out toward the snowcapped mountains.

When I reach the ice, I skid to a hard stop. Before, I would have quickened my pace and leaped forward, landing on the glassy surface. Bending my knees to create momentum, I would've skidded across eternity, spreading my arms wide and letting the wind freeze my nose and the tears on my cheeks.

Now, the icy lake looms like a pit of darkness, a pit of death.

I kneel down and place my hand on the ice. *Kyra…*

Most of the ice lies undisturbed, with only the barest hint of snow. The wind is too strong here to keep a decent snow cover. There are small cracks, but the only weak spots are the ones we create ourselves, with fishing drills or axes.

I hesitate. There is no way to quietly slip under this ice. The only way to do so is purposefully.

I trek along the edge of the lake to the dock and hoist myself up. In the winter, Kyra and I used to walk from one side of the lake to the other. Today, I'm the only one here. I might as well be the only person on earth, as quiet as it is.

I cannot believe that she died here. I don't want to believe that she died here.

On days when Kyra spiraled deep into depression, she would tell me that she just wanted everything to stop. To not be anymore, to cease to exist, as the only relief from those intense lows. But she never should have been in the position to act on that. Even when she struggled with her medication, she felt immeasurably better with it. Kyra's parents and Rowanne should've looked out for her. I would've reached out if I'd known. If I'd read the despair in her letters.

If I'd responded to her letters.

I would've...

The dock behind me creaks with footsteps, but when I turn, no one is there.

I'm alone—and I'm too much company for myself.

When I turn back to the lake, the snow blows away and the ice becomes as clear as glass. Underneath it float constellations of pink flowers. And I lose my breath at the thought of Kyra's lifeless, frozen body.

I *was* her friend, and she was mine. We were best friends long before we tried to be girlfriends, and best friends long after.

MEMORIES OF INFINITY

A YEAR AND A HALF BEFORE

UNLIKE MOST OF MY CLASSMATES, I NEVER HAD CRUSHES. I didn't understand what all the fuss was about, no matter how much Kyra tried to explain. I didn't see the appeal of Kyra's favorite actors, who she thought were hot. I barely remembered their names. My heart didn't flutter at the sight of a cute guy—or girl—smiling.

The only time I ever fell head over heels in love was at St. James, when Eileen took me to soccer practice. Except I fell in love with the game, not with the players.

But at the end of summer, when the nights were

lengthening and the air was growing colder, Kyra and I sat in her room. She laughed at a joke I'd made. She was half staring into some distant future as she braided a strand of hair.

"Mom told me that Mrs. Robinson is making her rhubarb crumble again," she said. "Maybe we should head over there tomorrow. Offer to help get her garden winter ready. Hope for a bite to eat."

Mrs. Robinson's garden and her rhubarb crumble were legendary in Lost. The rhubarb signaled the end of summer, and the recipe was older than the town itself, although we all secretly thought Mrs. Robinson was too. The woman was as resilient as the trees. At ninety-eight, she had no family to take care of her, but she still patched up her home and tended to her garden. At least, she did on the days that her arthritis released its claw-like grip on her hands.

Other days, Lost took care of her garden for her.

Mrs. Robinson was happy to see us. Unlike most others in town, she loved Kyra's company. She said that Kyra had a storyteller's soul and a gardener's hands, and that Kyra understood her land better than anyone else.

Earlier that week, Piper and Sam had already gone through the extensive garden to remove crop residues, but the frames and trellises, used for roses and vines and other climbers, still needed to be removed.

We spent a few hours deconstructing the frames and

carefully storing them in a raggedy shed that never saw the love the garden did. As Kyra and I worked, our hands touched. More, I thought, than they usually did.

Under Mrs. Robinson's direction, we used pitchforks to cover the plots of land with a thick layer of hay, like a scratchy yellow blanket. By the time we finished, our conversation had dwindled, the labor making our breathing heavy, but my arms felt even heavier. Right when I decided I'd never be able to lift my arms again, Kyra started laughing. She spread her arms and fell back in the hay, which, for all its thickness, barely cushioned her fall. She picked a stalk and chewed on it, glancing at me, her eyes sparkling. I lay down next to her with a little more care.

She rolled over on her side, more straw clinging to her hair. "There'll be flowers here again this spring. And roses come summer. Can you imagine it?"

I remembered this year's garden, and last year's. I didn't want to think too hard about next year's because that meant the start of senior year and college decisions. But Kyra's fingers twitched. She took in the different plots, as if she were already picturing the future garden. She loved exploring the possibilities of the world she knew.

Maybe that was why I felt beautiful when she smiled at me. The sun felt hotter. The hay tickled my back, and the sensation crept all the way along my spine, settling in my stomach.

I pushed myself up on one arm, and on impulse, I reached out and wove my fingers through hers.

She nibbled at her lower lip as a question appeared in her eyes.

I inched closer.

She leaned closer too.

I didn't know what I was doing. I'd never kissed anyone or been kissed before, and I always glanced away when other people made out. But seeing her there made me want to be closer to her than the love and friendship we already shared. I pressed my lips against hers and waited.

She paused, then smiled against my lips. When she opened her mouth and leaned in farther, she was hesitant and careful. Tender. Curious. Exploring.

The kiss tasted of hay and earth and salt and the tangy end of summer. It wasn't fireworks, like one of the girls at school claimed. Maybe it was spectacularly right.

But not for me.

I pulled away. And she crumpled.

Does St. James have legends and myths? Secret societies that meet once a month in the chapel? Ghosts that haunt the dorms?

Lost has created new legends since you left.

It's such a human thing to do. We tell stories about what we don't understand. I just never considered what it would be like to be at the heart of one of those stories. I want to study myths, not star in one.

IN THE COMPANY OF OTHERS

I WANDER BACK TO THE HENDERSONS' WHEN TWILIGHT gives way to dusk. Mrs. H is preparing dinner, while Mr. H and Sheriff Flynn meet in Mr. H's study. Mr. Sarin has gone back to the apartment he's renting on the other side of town to have dinner with his son. Another stranger.

I curl up on the sofa in the living room and cling to a sports book I brought with me. I can't focus on the words. I try to ignore the framed photos and Kyra's painting, but I can't stop stealing glances.

When Mr. H and Sheriff Flynn return to the living room, still talking business, I lose focus entirely and give my curiosity free rein. Mr. H would never talk business in front of Kyra. He wanted to be home when he was home—not to spend those rare days when he wasn't traveling focused on what was happening across the state. But that's hardly relevant anymore.

And his talk is not merely of business, but of a future for Lost.

"—a financial injection into the mineral mining industry will create more jobs in the surrounding area and boost the local economy," Mr. H says.

Sheriff Flynn nods. "With a focus on the right projects, Sarin's money may help revitalize Lost."

The more Mr. H and Sheriff Flynn talk, the more I forget my book.

Apparently this area is still rich—not with gold, but with metals. Wolfram. Bismuth. Both rare and valuable, and no one has ever tried to exploit those resources here. Mr. H's mining company doesn't have the researchers or the experience, but apparently Mr. Sarin's arrival brings both to town. Renewed mining would mean a new and steady source of income. It would create an influx of workers and services. It would strengthen the local economy. Life isn't impossible in Lost by any means, but it isn't easy. If the mine reopened, the resulting financial boom would mean everything for the town.

Still. Kyra always said that there was more to mining than the riches, and there was a world to consider beyond the borders of Lost. Mining damaged the land. It would affect Native life and culture around us. Did Mr. H think about that too? "What about the environmental risks?"

But with those five words, they both turn to me, and the conversation extinguishes itself.

"The plans are still in early stages," is all Mr. H says before he abruptly excuses himself to the kitchen.

I place my book on the couch. "Sheriff?"

"As Joe says, planning is under way. We'll consider what we must for our community." Sheriff Flynn's voice is flat. He perches on one of the armchairs and rolls his shoulders back. His hands are balled into fists. "In any case, it's good to see you *visiting* Lost, Corey. How's your mom?"

I'm momentarily thrown by the change of subject. "Good. She likes her job at the hospital."

The lines in his forehead ease a bit. Once upon a time, he and my mom grew up together, and they've always remained good friends. "Is she still working too hard?"

"I don't think Mom knows what rest means." The corner of my mouth tugs up. "But at least she isn't traveling so much anymore."

He shakes his head. "She never could stay within these borders. It surprised me when she came back after college. I never expected her to stay."

I wondered about that sometimes, what Kyra and I would do after college. Before Mom got her job offer in Winnipeg, I might have daydreamed about life in Fairbanks or even Chile, but I'd never *really* considered leaving Lost forever. And as far as I knew, Mom had always planned to stay in Lost too. Even after Dad left. But Kyra… "I always thought Kyra would escape too."

And with that, Sheriff Flynn's face hardens again. "Kyra belonged here."

Except she didn't. I glance at the painting. I can't talk to the Hendersons about Kyra's death, and part of me still can't believe that she's really gone. More than that, I don't *want* to believe that she chose to end her own life. "Sheriff, I wanted to ask you—"

"I'd rather you didn't," he interrupts me curtly.

"But I want to understand what happened."

He lowers his voice so the Hendersons won't overhear him. "She drowned, Corey. When she was missing from her room, her father went looking for her and found her body under the ice. That's all there is to it, and you should know better than to pry into other people's business. Your mother raised you better than that."

I mutter something about what my mother would think if she were here. "But the lake is frozen. The ice is inches thick. You know as well as I do—"

"It's always possible to find weak spots." Sheriff Flynn's mouth thins. "Lost has changed since you left. But you have too. If you want to continue calling yourself her friend, then you'd better respect this community. Kyra would've wanted that. We respected her. We found meaning together. We were here for her."

What he doesn't say is clear. *We were here for her. And you weren't.*

Sheriff Flynn gets to his feet, momentarily towering over me. But it's not his physical presence that makes me feel small. It's the anger that radiates from him. After Dad left, he would check up on Mom, Luke, and me, to make sure that we were provided for. He would play ball with my brother and me. Now he turns his back to me.

All I can think to whisper is, "I miss my best friend, Sheriff."

But instead of acknowledging my words, he shrugs them off and walks back toward Mr. H's study.

....

My attempts at conversation during dinner don't fare any better. Before we eat, Mrs. H asks for a moment of silence in remembrance of Kyra, but the last thing I need is more time alone with my thoughts.

Despite planning not to discuss business in front of me, that's exactly what Mr. H and the sheriff do, though in hushed tones so soft their words are nearly indiscernible.

I hardly have an appetite, so I keep pushing vegetables around on my plate. And though I try to make conversation with Mrs. H, her welcome has fizzled out. She won't allow any questions. Instead, she twists all of my questions into ones of her own.

"How did Kyra find her place here?" I ask.

"She realized that she needed to stop fighting. It's hard finding one's place when you're so young. I imagine you must've had quite a transition these past few months. You don't belong here anymore, but you don't belong in your new town yet either. Your mother told me about your boarding school. St. James, is it? She said you were playing soccer. Tell me about that."

Once more, I try, "What *happened*?"

"Oh, Corey. It was her time. Every story must end, because the ending gives the story meaning. Kyra knew that. She foresaw it. She foresaw a great many things." She folds her hands and slowly exhales, stealing a glance of her own at the painting in the living room. "I know it's hard to understand, but we learned to accept it."

"What do you mean? If she was suicidal, she needed help."

"No." Mrs. H shakes her head. She closes her eyes, but instead of grief, a look of peace comes over her features. "You'll come to see it too. Her death was inevitable, and so be it."

I bite my lip until I taste blood. *Of course Kyra's death wasn't inevitable. How can they accept that?*

Mr. H turns to his wife and places a hand over her folded hands. His broad shoulders sag. And all I can think about is how when Kyra was small, she used to love sitting on his shoulders, seeing the world from up high.

"She's right, Corey," he says. "By the time we—I— found her, it was too late. We were too late. But we are comforted by what Kyra would say: that every story must end. It's death, after all, that gives our lives meaning."

PHONE CALL

"How was your flight? How is it to be back home?"

"I'm not sure this is home anymore, Eileen. I feel like a stranger."

"In what way?"

"Well, people keep telling me that I am. They call me 'outsider.'"

"Corey? Are you okay?"

"E, did I ever tell you that you're the only one at St. James who even knows about Kyra?"

"Really? Why?"

"Because it was hard to talk about her. You were the only one who I thought would understand. You never judged. I carried her with me. My best friend. I didn't want people to judge me like they did in Lost, except now I wish I had talked about her more. We had so many stories to share."

"Oh, Cor."

"Out of the two of us, Kyra was the one who believed in better times. I put my faith in science and stars, but she put her faith in stories, which could turn regular people into extraordinary ones. When she had her first manic episodes, they didn't consume her—they helped her create. We dubbed them 'hero days.' They were some of the best times we had in Lost Creek. And now we have no days left at all."

"At least you're there to say goodbye."

"Yeah…"

"Would you rather not have gone?"

"No, I'm glad to be here. I just… They say she was happy. That it was 'her time.'"

"What does that mean?"

"I don't know. It wasn't her time. It wasn't. But everyone accepts her death as if it were inevitable."

"It's not uncommon for someone with bipolar disorder to be suicidal."

"In that case, shouldn't they have tried to help her? She told me that she was lonely. In her last letters, she was upset, but she didn't say why. But I didn't think… I didn't even write back to her. I was too preoccupied with finding my place at St. James. But she promised to wait for me. She was waiting for me. I have to believe that. I need to believe that."

"Do you think her death could've been an accident?"

"White Wolf Lake is frozen solid in winter. There are few holes and even fewer weak spots. We both grew up here. Kyra would have known what to look for. And I…"

"What?"

"Nothing. Never mind."

"Corey?"

"Even at her darkest, Kyra was so curious about the world. There was so much she wanted to learn and read. She was scared, and lonely, but she lived fiercely."

"Even people who love life can be depressed, Corey. You don't know what happened after you left."

"I have four days to find out."

"What do you think you'll find?"

"Her side of the story. She cared so deeply about stories. I owe it to her to find and protect hers."

FORESEEN AND FORETOLD

AFTER DINNER, I WANDER BACK INTO TOWN. CALLING Eileen helped settle the heartache a little, but I need some fresh air. I cross to the other side of Lost. It takes me less time than it would to cross St. James's campus. On Main Street, I pause in front of Claja.

This place belongs to the adults in the evenings, but I sneak in anyway. Maybe I'll find someone who is happy to see me.

The pub is dimly lit, but I spot Piper sitting at the counter. Next to her sits a boy our age with spiky black hair and dark, golden skin. I've never seen him before.

After a moment's hesitation, Piper waves me over. The boy turns and his eyes flash in recognition.

I make my way over, passing the handful of tables. I glance around to see if Sam is anywhere, but there are no other teens here. Only Mr. Lucas, the manager. Jan from the grocery store. Old Mr. Wilde, one of the miners who retired here. Three empty glasses stand in front of him, and he's working his way through a fourth. No one calls out in greeting, but the buzz of voices grows quieter.

I sidle up next to Piper and the boy. "Hi?"

"You must be Corey. Come, join us." His voice is tinged with an English accent. "I'm Roshan."

"Have we met?"

"I feel like I know you. She spoke of you often." His face is solemn, but he ventures a smile.

I sit on the stool next to him, while Piper orders me a hot chocolate. "You knew Kyra?" I ask.

"We were friends, right at the end. Like you were."

I muster a broken smile and some weight falls off my shoulders. "You're the first to acknowledge that I was her friend. Everyone else seems to think I'm an intruder here."

Piper scoffs, but Roshan ignores it. "That seems to be the way of Lost. It does not take kindly to changes, whether it's people going"—he gestures to me—"or coming." He points a thumb at himself. "Give them some time. They will grow used to you once more. They will remember how much Kyra meant to you, and you to Kyra."

It's weird to have a stranger tell me about the town where I lived almost all of my life, but I take his words gladly. Still, "I won't be staying long. I'm only here for a couple of days. To say goodbye—and find out what happened."

Piper hasn't said anything so far, but now she finally bites. "Find out what happened? What, like an investigation?"

I shrug. "Kyra and I, we had an agreement. We would always, always wait for each other. No one else looked out for her—and she looked out for me. Nothing would have changed that." *Except my leaving. And every letter I ignored.* I wrap my trembling hands around the mug of hot chocolate. "No one was kind to her while she was alive, and now everyone sings her praises."

"Isn't that what you're supposed to do?" Piper asks. "Not speak ill of the dead?"

"She deserved the truth, not hypocrisy."

"What is the truth, then?" she asks, mildly.

"I don't know," I admit.

Piper shakes her head. "Walk around Lost tomorrow. Not to investigate, but to listen. Because we changed, and the truth is that Lost is doing better than it has in a long time. We have hope."

"You can't have hope with grief," I say.

Roshan shakes his head, and a shadow passes over his

75

face. A distant memory. Then one corner of his mouth curls up. "You can. They're not mutually exclusive. You can grieve and still hope. You can mourn as you celebrate."

"We don't mourn," Piper cuts in, serenely. "We just celebrate. That's what Kyra would have wanted."

I turn the mug in my hands, so I won't reach out and shake her. "How can you possibly know what Kyra would've wanted? Did she *foresee* it?"

"She foretold it," Piper replies. "Come." She grabs my hand and pulls me off my stool, toward the back wall of the room. A group congregating by the bar steps out of the way to let us pass. When Piper turns up the lights, I'm overwhelmed. The entire wall is covered with Kyra's drawings, paintings, and sketches. Maps of the mine. The spa, covered in flowers. Sam standing at the edge of town. Mr. Sarin and Mr. Henderson walking down Main.

And in the farthest corner, a colorful rendition of tonight. Three teens, sitting at the counter, drinking hot chocolate. Piper. Roshan. And me.

"With her art, she showed us the future. And once you understand that, you'll find Kyra's truth."

WHISPERS IN THE NIGHT

THAT NIGHT, THE FLOORBOARDS ON THE OTHER SIDE OF the wall protest. Kyra's room is locked and empty. But I recognize her gait.

I sit up.

My heart skips, jolting against my rib cage. The closet door moves in a breeze, and the sound of laughter swirls around me once more. It's closer now.

It's in Kyra's room.

I wrap a hoodie around my shoulders and climb out of bed.

Outside, the wind picks up and hail pelts the windows. I consider switching on the main lights because the lamp on the nightstand barely illuminates the bed, but I don't want to break the spell.

Corey. The voice sounds distant, twisted, as if we're standing on opposite sides of the lake's dark waters. The air is cold as ice.

I know, I *know*, the next time the door to the closet inches open, Kyra will step out. I draw in a breath and my hand edges toward the door.

I open the door and stare into darkness. The wooden planks that form the back of the closet are gone, but there is a doorway to Kyra's room.

A chill settles into my bones. Kyra loved horror stories, but I do not. I'll take good old rational science over horror any day. When the wind roars along the cabin, it's all I can do to keep from screaming in fright. I snap on the lights before I can talk myself out of it again.

Science doesn't explain why the passage to Kyra's room is open. Why I'm crawling through it. As soon as Mr. Henderson finds out that Kyra's room was breached, he'll board it up again. This may be my only chance to get in.

The darkness feels oppressive. The silence even worse.

I grab my phone from my hoodie and toggle to the flashlight mode. My heart is beating out of control. The beam of light is both a comfort and a terror. I'm not prepared for what I'll see—or for what lurks just beyond the light.

Someone laughs. Low and far away. Or maybe it's the wind.

Slowly, I pan the light from one wall to the next. My hand trembles.

On my far left, the wall is covered with the very same drawings and paintings that decorate Kyra's door. Superheroes and comic-book scenes among panoramas of Alaska. Another wall is covered with faces. Half-drawn portraits. Ink and paint and pencil. A hundred eyes decorate the wall, and they are all watching me.

We sat on this floor for hours, doing our homework.

I move the beam of light along Kyra's bed. The covers are thrown across the mattress haphazardly, as if she just got up and could return any moment. Or as if someone or something is lying underneath them.

I hold my breath. I could crouch down and look under the bed, but my hands shake. My courage doesn't extend that far. I can't fight off monsters and nightmares. I never could.

I step back and settle the beam on Kyra's desk. A bright red shirt hangs across the desk chair. It's the same shirt she wore the last time I saw her. I take a measured step closer and run my hand over the fabric.

The light hits the curtain on the window over her desk. I gasp. The curtains have been cut to shreds—and they sway in a nonexistent breeze.

My cell phone light flickers. It takes everything I have not to turn and bolt. There must be an explanation for all this, although I can't seem to think of one. Instead, I step closer to her desk, but what I see doesn't make me feel any better. Shredded essays. Unfinished scripts and storyboards. Crumpled papers. A broken pen. A book soaked in paint.

I touch the paint. My fingertips come back pink.

I hold up the light to the bookshelves adjacent to the desk. Most of her books are gone. What's left has been shredded too. Her entire collection of folktales and legends. Her treasured copies of the Edda, prose and poetry. The books her grandfather wrote. Her collection on the history of storytelling. All destroyed.

This isn't right. Even in her darkest moments, Kyra would never be so careless. She wouldn't be concerned about the curtains, but she was meticulous about her stories and her studies.

This isn't right.

I edge forward and pick up one of the papers. When I brush the bookshelf, my fingers get coated thick with dust. Upon closer inspection, I see that the floor is covered in a layer of dust too. I can see my footprints behind me. If Kyra was alive a few days ago, she wasn't here. Aside from the fresh paint, this room hasn't been lived in for weeks, maybe months.

There might be more clues here, but the curtains move and the papers rustle again in some imaginary draft, and I've had enough.

Corey. A whisper tickles my ear.

I swirl. My phone nearly slips from my fingers. The beam of light streaks across the wall. *Nothing. Emptiness.*

This room used to be the safest place on earth. *Not anymore.* I beeline back to the passage and Kyra's studio, locking the closet door behind me for good measure.

Only when I'm huddled in my bed, safely under the covers, do I look at the torn page that I hold, written in Kyra's uneven hand.

Dear Corey,

I'm scared. I'm scared. I'm scared. I'm scared. I'm scared. I'm scared.

~~I'm scared. I'm scared. I'm scared. I'm scared. I'm scared. I'm scared.~~

I'm waiting.

DAY TWO

ASTRONOMICAL TWILIGHT

THE CABIN IS DARK AND STILL WHEN I WAKE FROM A
restless sleep. The deep silence settles into my bones.
Back at St. James's, there would be the sound of fifteen
girls getting up and starting their day, arguing over the
bathrooms, sharing each other's clothes. I miss the laughter. I miss the smell of freshly brewed coffee. I miss
Eileen's pen scratching in her notebook as she plots the
next great Canadian novel, while the rest of us are barely
awake enough to figure out breakfast.

I miss Kyra.

She would've liked Eileen and her stories. Eileen
would've liked Kyra and her fascination with narrative.

I was going to introduce them when Kyra came to visit me over the summer, like we'd planned. Before...

She died.

Her loss hits me anew. I still can't accept it. I want answers.

So I snuggle into my jeans and bunny boots and pull on a sweater with long sleeves I can hide my hands in. It's early, and I'm sure Mrs. H will be preparing breakfast, but I don't want to go inside the main house yet. If Mrs. H can't give me answers, maybe Mrs. Morden, at the post office, will. Or Mrs. Robinson, who took to Kyra more than anyone else in town did.

I grab my parka and hat from my backpack, then wrap a scarf around my neck and pull on my mittens. It's a quiet ritual, this creation of another layer of skin, and for the first time since I've been back, I feel Alaskan again.

At my desk, I grab Kyra's letter and stare at it.

I'm waiting.

Where were you waiting, Kyr? If you weren't here, where do I find you?

I stuff the letter into a pocket. It's a tangible reminder of her. I want to keep it close.

Lights are on in the Hendersons' kitchen as I slip through the garden. It's almost eight, but I can just start to make out the difference between the trees and the sky. Back home, this is the time classes start.

Back home.

I shrug my parka higher. This *is* back home.

It'll be another hour or two before the sun will tease the horizon. Real sunlight won't happen until almost eleven, but Lost doesn't shy away from the darkness.

When I make it to the town square, where Main Street intersects with two smaller roads, the fishermen have already left, but the handful of stores—the post office, the grocery store, the doctor's office—are still closed. The street lights shine dimly. And the only sound is that of the wind whistling past the buildings. Lost looks like a ghost town.

Even in a small town like this, the quiet feels out of place. I pause at the corner where, one summer, Kyra decided to settle on one of the benches in front of the grocery store, a notebook in hand.

She told me she wanted to record the stories of Lost. The first day, people stared at her oddly. The second, most gave her only passing glances.

By the third day, everyone in Lost had passed her at least half a dozen times, and they seemed to have forgotten about her entirely. "It gives me a chance to look at Lost from a different perspective," she said. "When people forget you, you hear—and see—all sorts of things."

But when I quizzed her about what she'd discovered, she wouldn't tell.

I lean against one of the street lights, and I feel like an observer now too. Though I'm not sure what to observe, except for the magenta ribbons that dance in the breeze.

But the longer I look, the more I notice.

First, the mural on the side of the post office. Even in the dim light, I recognize the muted colors of spring. The first bright sunrise. The promise of ice breaking up and the weather warming. It's so hopeful that it makes me want to cry or rage at the unfairness of it all. This is clearly one of Kyra's paintings—and she won't see another spring.

I look away, and cold pricks up my arms.

Silhouettes darken the windows of almost every single house. Everywhere I turn, everywhere, they stare. Yesterday I thought that Lost Creek looked like a collection of dollhouses; today I've found the dolls.

A shiver runs down my spine. I take a step back toward the Hendersons'. Someone out of sight starts humming like the girl at the airport. A few bars into the tune, a scream interrupts the song. The sound is shrill and angry, like the screeching of an eagle. But is it a bird or a human? I can't tell.

I freeze and Lost falls silent. Waiting.

I take another step and the shrieking starts again. My heart pounds. I stop. For the first time in seventeen years, I understand what Kyra meant when she said that she felt claustrophobic here.

Inside the post office, a light switches on. Mrs. Morden, Piper's grandmother, steps out to hang her fake potted plant next to the door. It's as if she breaks the spell. The shadows retreat from the windows.

My balled fists relax, and I roll my shoulders, fending off the cold. My movement startles Mrs. Morden. She squints into the early dawn. "Who's there?"

I come closer, my feet scrunching the freshly fallen snow. "It's me, Corey. Morning, Mrs. Morden."

"*Corey.*"

"I wanted to come say hi." I smile, but she offers no friendly return.

After a moment, she nods toward the door. "Coffee's brewing. Make yourself at home." She sounds resigned, and I deflate. Mrs. Morden is always happy to see everyone. I thought she would be happy to see me.

I follow her into the post office. From the wood paneling on the walls to the old-fashioned service windows, it looks—I imagine—exactly like it did a hundred-something years ago. Of course, Lost Creek never needed more than one clerk in the post office.

Even the coffee machine, brewing inside the small office, looks like an antique. It sounds like one too. I grab a chipped mug and a cookie from one of the shelves and wait for the coffee to finish brewing.

My gaze settles on the desk. This used to be Mr.

Morden's desk. He passed away seventeen years ago, but Mrs. Morden never cleaned it out. It looked like he simply stepped away for a moment. She kept his books stacked next to his mug and his coat draped across the chair. She would dust it and mind it and pretend he was still here.

Whenever Kyra and I visited, we would surreptitiously check to see if any of his belongings had moved. He still had such a presence that we were convinced that his ghost haunted this place.

But now, the desk is empty. The only evidence of old Mr. Morden is a portrait that hangs over his desk.

"That's one of Kyra's too," I blurt from the office doorway.

Mrs. Morden fusses in the main room—straightening the priority box display and readjusting the stamp machine. All the while, she manages to avoid looking at me. "It was time for a change."

"Did she foresee it?" I snap. It's the same question that I asked Piper, and I can't keep the bitterness out of my voice.

"I recognized and accepted her gift." She says nothing more.

When the silence lengthens into discomfort, I pour a second cup of coffee, for Mrs. Morden, and place myself directly in front of her, grasping for a simpler conversation. "I hope you don't mind. I ate one of your cookies. I haven't had breakfast yet."

Before, she would have laughed. She would have harrumphed. She would have commented on the forwardness of today's youth and the negative influence of the outside world.

Now, she only shakes her head and accepts the mug in silence.

I want to ask her how she is, how business is, what all the latest Lost Creek gossip is, like Kyra always used to do when we would come for our mail. What comes out instead is, "Why won't anyone speak to me?"

She starts at that, almost as surprised as I am. "You know how it is, dear. You're an outsider. And Lost Creek does not take kindly to strangers."

WE CAN BE HEROES

TWO YEARS BEFORE

"MY MIND IS A STRANGER TO ME," KYRA SAID. SHE HAD just come back from her session with Rowanne, and she exuded restless tension.

"What do you mean?" I asked.

She closed my books, moved my homework to the side of the desk, and tossed me my coat. "Let's go to the spa."

I swallowed a flash of annoyance. We'd claimed the spa as our own last summer, when Kyra was traveling back and forth between Lost and Fairbanks for diagnostic appointments. Our parents had always told us that the building was too old and dangerous to be a playground, but it proved perfect as a hideout when Kyra didn't want to face Lost's questions and judgment.

That summer, she'd told me, "You know, this building would be a fantastic secret lair or superhero headquarters. Even with the work Aaron did to restore the rooms and windows, it still looks ancient and decrepit. It's the perfect facade."

"Will we be heroes then?" I'd asked.

"No, but we'll be safe."

But this day, she didn't speak again until we had climbed through the spa's kitchen window. She led me through the building to the bedrooms on the second floor. The rooms on the north side had narrow balconies, and one of them gave us a magnificent view of the green woods, the bright blue sky, and the snowcapped mountains in the distance.

Kyra pulled out the stash of chocolate we'd hidden under a loose floorboard. "Rowanne wants me to try mood stabilizers."

I broke off a piece of chocolate. "For the mania?"

"Yeah."

"How do you feel about that?"

She shrugged. "If it helps, I'll do anything."

I blundered into my next question. "Won't you miss it? Not the depression, but the energy?"

On days when the manic episodes didn't completely overwhelm her, they boosted her. She'd paint for hours. She'd do her homework in a hurry. She'd be intensely happy and up for any adventure.

On those days, we'd spend our time at the spa, and we *were* heroes. We'd make up the most outrageous stories and act them out. We'd go hunting for secret passages. We'd play hide and seek with shadows.

Those were good days.

"Who's to say that's my mania and not me?" Kyra asked.

I opened my mouth and closed it again.

"My mind is a stranger to me," she repeated, harsher this time. "I can't control what it does. I know I can't change that, but I can try to find a better way to live with it."

CONVERSATIONS

I RECOIL. "I'M NO MORE A STRANGER THAN YOU ARE, OR than Kyra was, or anyone else. Lost Creek is our home."

Mrs. Morden's eyes flash at the mention of Kyra. "Perhaps it was once." She places the dustcloth on the corner of the counter by the window and shakes her head. "Night and day don't wait for us. You knew Lost as it used to be, but we've changed since you left. It's not an accusation, simply a matter of fact. It is how it is, and so be it."

So be it. Those words are beginning to sound like an echo. I wasn't here. I should've been here. Mrs. Morden may not mean them as an accusation, but they certainly feel like one.

"It's only been seven months," I protest weakly.

"And lifetimes."

"Then tell me how Lost has changed," I demand, and to my horror, my voice cracks. I've never cried in front of anyone, except for Kyra. "Because my best friend is gone, and no one will even let me mourn. My best friend is gone, and all anyone can talk about are her paintings. I want to understand how she lived and how she died."

"Do you really?" Mrs. Morden folds her hands together, and the gesture is so like my math teacher's at St. James that I'm momentarily disoriented.

I nod.

"Kyra and Lost bonded over art. Kyra started drawing and painting more after you left. I'm sure you've seen her art around town. She found a way to express herself, which helped us all communicate. She started using the old spa as her studio."

"Is that where she stayed then?"

"Kyra didn't sleep out in the cold, if that's what you're asking," Mrs. Morden snaps. "She stayed there. She had a comfortable room and lots of space to create. And you know how much she loved that building."

I know that she went to the spa to *escape*, to find peace away from the town's prying eyes.

"Kyra and I talked a lot. She was always curious to hear what Lost was like when I was your age because it was so different back then. We talked about the stories my grandfather told me, the stories her grandfather told her, and the gossip I heard from customers. She told me how she thought Lost would change—and grow."

I nod. That I can imagine. Kyra always wanted to know the stories that shaped the people around her. She always wanted to understand why people were the way they were. Outside of her episodes, she thrived on company—and on their stories. Like here, *the story of a haunted post office*.

"The more time I spent with Kyra, the more I thought that she would've gotten along well with my late husband. Wilfred saw to the heart of people too, and they were both so easy to talk to. One day we talked about him for hours, and it almost felt like having him here with us. After all those years… It felt as if he were home. A few days later, Kyra had turned one of my old photos of Wilfred into a painting." She nods at the wall. Kyra had made Mr. Morden look older and weathered, like his widow.

With her free hand, Mrs. Morden pulls a tissue from her sleeve and dabs at her eyes. "I never realized how talented she was until that moment. I never stopped mourning my husband, Corey, but because of her painting, I can imagine that he saw more of this world than he did. Her painting gives me peace."

"I wish she'd gotten to see more of the world too," I say.

"Corey?" A hint of urgency creeps into Mrs. Morden's

voice. "You mustn't worry about her. We were here for her. We provided her with everything she needed. Lost doesn't take well to change, but we learned to understand her. She was *happy*."

"How can you possibly know that?" It takes everything I have to keep my voice even and calm. Kyra escaped to the spa when she didn't feel comfortable in Lost. She painted when she couldn't calm her mind. And she *died*.

"You two used to come here together. She didn't stop coming after you moved away. We saw each other often, and she made new friends. After she moved into the spa, I went to visit her, at least once a week, and she'd come into town whenever she wanted." Mrs. Morden reaches out and grabs my hand. Her fingers are stiff and cold. "Kyra found her connection to the people in town through her art. She listened to our requests and our petitions, and she painted dozens of illustrations for us. She spread happiness. Kyra finding a place here was a sign to all of us that Lost can change—and change for the better. After all those years, she'd finally come home to us, and we to her. She was at peace."

"Then why did she take her own life?"

"Because no star can burn forever."

I still have so many questions, but the one that tumbles out is, "Did she ever talk about me?"

Mrs. Morden smiles, even as her eyes become watery.

She squeezes my hand as hard as her old muscles will let her. Then she goes to her desk and shuffles through the papers in her drawer. She produces a postcard, which she hands to me. Kyra's telltale handwriting covers the back of it. "With every letter she sent out, dear, and the ones she didn't," Mrs. Morden said to me. "She talked about you whenever she could."

THE CHOICES WE MAKE

TWO MONTHS BEFORE

NOA BARGED INTO MY DORM ROOM WITHOUT KNOCKING and dumped the mail on my bed. "Can I borrow this issue when you're done?" she asked, gesturing to my copy of *World Soccer*.

I glanced up from my physics homework. "Sure. If you want, you can read it first."

"Nah." She held up an armful of comics—the latest *Ms. Marvel* the only visible title. "Eloi provided me with plenty of reading. I'm good for now."

I smirked. "My brother would get along so well with yours."

"Next Family Day?"

"We should ask Eileen to introduce them to her table-top game club. Luke would be all over that."

Eileen appeared in the doorway. "Who would be all over what?" She spotted the mail delivery. "Ooh, you got the new *World Soccer!*" She fell onto my bed and started to read.

"We're showing our geeky brothers around St. James on Family Day. You should take them along to Boarding Games," Noa said. With no other place to sit, she leaned against my desk.

"So now I'm the resident nerd?" Eileen propped herself up on one elbow and pushed a black curl behind her ear.

"Nerd, scribbler, dorm grandma, decent midfielder." Noa ticked off the list on her fingers.

"Dorm grandma?" Eileen sat up and her dark brown eyes flashed. "Excuse you, I'm six months younger than you are. I'm also a better player, and my writing happens to be *art.*"

With an inward smile and an outward sigh of resignation, I reached for my physics book. With the two of them in that mood, I knew I'd get nothing done.

At the sound of the book slamming shut, both Eileen

and Noa looked at me, mischief in their eyes. They couldn't be more dissimilar if they tried. Eileen was small and lanky, one of the few Black girls at St. James, and one of the most tactical players I knew. Noa, white and with long blond hair, was tall and broad, a strong striker whose physicality had helped our team on numerous occasions.

But despite their differences, their matching smiles were both aimed at me.

"Speaking of the beautiful game," Eileen said, "we should go to the fields." She got up and leaned theatrically toward me. "Coach brought Maddy along," she mock-whispered, loudly enough for Noa to hear. "She's home for a couple of days before her team's midseason training retreat. She got picked to start varsity for her first game, so she's now a very desirable collegiate athlete." She drew out the last four words.

Noa blushed furiously and made an unconvincing excuse before bolting to change her clothes.

I grinned at Eileen. "You're evil and I love it."

"I know." She picked up a letter from Kyra and handed it to me. "If you want to stay in and read first... Maddy will be here for a while. Plenty of time to bother Noa later."

I accepted the letter and stared at Kyra's looping handwriting. It was such a familiar sight, such a reminder of Lost. I wanted to know what she had to say, and I had so much to tell her too. *I fit in here, Kyr. I have friends. Sports. Can you imagine, me, an athlete? I'm so different here.*

I never knew how to start explaining that to her.

I opened my desk drawer and placed the letter on top of the stack of her other letters. Some opened, some unopened. All unanswered.

I bit my lip. "I'll read it tonight."

Eileen tilted her head. "Are you sure?"

"And miss those first awkward conversations? No chance."

"C'mon then." Eileen hooked her arm through mine and drew me out of the room. As always, her easy camaraderie felt both comforting and exhilarating.

I hadn't kept Kyra a secret from the others on purpose; it just happened. I came to St. James thinking that I would be treated with the same hostility that Lost Creek shows newcomers, but the girls accepted me without question. It was easy to belong here. And I could start fresh, without the burden of who I was in Lost, where everyone knew me and had known me since birth. Everyone here was new, and every day felt like an adventure. I didn't want to lose that high. So I let myself get swept away by life at St. James, with its clearer borders and softer rules. Far away from Kyra.

With a whisper of guilt, I closed the door behind me.

A NEW LOST

WHEN I STEP OUT OF THE POST OFFICE, I FIND THAT Lost Creek has come to life. The shadows in the windows are gone. People are walking into the grocery store and running errands. I push my hands into my pockets and head to the far side of the building.

A mural covers the entire wall, depicting the Alaskan landscape in the brightest spring colors. A brilliant red sun. Azure sky. Magenta flowers. Neon green pine trees. The Gates of the Arctic National Park, with its snowcapped peaks, is in the distance. A river of multicolored envelopes streams from the upper-right corner to the bottom left. The painting is quintessentially Kyra.

It must have taken her days, if not longer. There is so much detail, and the more I look, the more I see. Piper and Tobias, standing in front of their grandmother's post office. A smiling Sam. Mrs. Robinson's gardens. A brightly colored Lost. An airplane at the strip. But also fully functional mines, with tall machinery on the hillside, surrounded by acres of blackened, industrial land.

My heart pounds. With trembling fingers, I trace the footpaths to White Wolf Lake, where I find the shadow under the ice.

Everywhere I turn, Kyra has left signs pointing to her death, well before she died. She knew what was going to happen. She told everyone. And no one made a move to stop her. *She foresaw, so they…let it happen?*

I can't bear to look at this mural any longer. I turn to the street. Lost Creek doesn't have a church, but everyone looks as if they're going to one anyway. On their parkas and winter coats, they all wear ribbons, the same black and magenta as the ribbons tied to their houses.

And their voices swirl around me.

You never cared enough.

You were never her friend.

The faces of friends morph into strangers and enemies. Why is my coming to say goodbye a bad thing? When did I become a threat? I don't understand, but I shrink away all the same.

Tomorrow, they'll pay their respects to a girl they never knew, a girl who somehow managed to find a central place in their lives.

Three men turn on to Main—Mr. H, Mr. Sarin, and Sheriff Flynn. None of them are dressed in black, but Mr. H wears his grief in the lines of his face and the hunch of his shoulders. Each has a salmonberry flower pinned to his coat. I shrink back into the shadows and listen as they pass by. They still talk about mining and investments and minerals, about renewing the future of Lost Creek, as a matter of prosperity.

And in the town where nothing ever changes, everything is changing.

It's for the better, I can almost hear Mrs. Morden say. *These changes give Lost a future*. And she's right.

New industry would mean a boost for everyone. The grocery store could expand. People could renovate instead of simply freshening their houses with paint, fixing broken roofs, putting away funds for hard times and once-faraway dreams.

But at what cost?

This change would be as sudden as a thunderstorm, and in Alaska, thunderstorms are rare and violent.

I turn, and my gaze meets Sam Flynn's. He leans against a building across the street, and he stares at me but makes no move to come closer. We were friendly, once. Not friends, exactly, but close nonetheless. Now...

Now I am lost too.

HAPPILY SOMETIMES

NINE MONTHS BEFORE

WE DANCED ON THE ICE.

It was shortly before breakup in the spring, when the Lyrid meteor shower lit up the sky. I'd been tracking meteor predictions, and when I told Kyra the peak night for viewing was supposed to be almost moonless, she decided we needed a celebration. On the nights when she couldn't paint and she wandered beyond the borders of Lost, she would gather flower petals to strew across town or try to build a bonfire to watch the fire dance. That night, she wanted to be the one dancing.

"The night is so dark," she said. "What if there is no dawn, and winter never ends? I want to take advantage of each and every moment."

"I think we can safely assume that the sun will rise in the morning, even if we don't see it."

The corner of her mouth crept up. "How can you know for sure?"

"I don't. But science does. So I trust that it will. And besides, with the Lyrids tonight, the darker the night sky is, the better our chance of seeing shooting stars," I told her.

So we sneaked out of the cabin when the Lyra constellation peeked out over the horizon, shortly before dawn, and walked onto the frozen surface of White Wolf Lake. I'd bundled up in my winter coat and extra scarves because the wind was fierce, but Kyra went out in a loose coat with pink flowers in her hair. The salmonberry bushes had started blossoming a few days ago, peeking out of the slowly melting snow, but where she'd picked fresh flowers in the middle of the night was beyond me. Wonder always followed Kyra like a curious pup, and I'd stopped questioning it long ago.

"So how do you want to celebrate?" I asked.

Kyra walked toward a clear spot near the lake's edge. The ice was still dark and thick but had started showing its first cracks. The surface reflected the skies above. A gust of wind swirled around us, whipping up the last of the snow cover. Kyra spread her arms wide and spun. "With stories, of course."

"You'll freeze to death. Zip up your coat," I said, and I tossed her the extra scarves I'd snatched from her room.

She rolled her eyes with a smile. And when she pulled me between the stars that shined on the ice, her hands were warm around mine. "Grandfather always said that stories are the heartbeat of the world, especially in Alaska. Stories shape us. They give meaning to the harshest winters and the longest summers."

Even though Kyra's family had been in Lost Creek since the town's beginnings, her grandfather had been an outsider at first. As a folklorist, he used to travel around to listen to and record the stories of the Koyukon Athabascan and the Iñupiat, the Yupik and the Haida. Though he had shared countless stories with Kyra, she would never share them with me. She said they hadn't been his stories to begin with, and the only way to understand those narratives was to respect and know the people they belonged to.

"Then what stories will you tell?" I asked.

"Ours. Lost Creek is full of stories too. Stories of love and secrets. Of friendship and survival. Of hate." She swallowed hard, as if thinking of a particular story. After a moment's pause, she said, "We live and create our own stories. The story of Sam, the sheriff's son who never smiles. The story of a haunted post office. The stories in the games your brother designs. The story of you and me and all of us on this stolen land. Don't you think our stories are what make us human?"

I mostly kept my eyes trained on the northeast, so I wouldn't miss the meteors, but at that remark, I turned back to her. "Wouldn't you prefer happier stories? Happily ever afters?"

"Would I?" Kyra's gaze settled on the distant night sky. "Think of your meteors. What if they aren't all science? What if the burning lights we see are spirits, falling back to earth? What if they're trying to return to their loved ones before they burn out? What if a falling star is a soul coming home, one last time?"

The differences between us were never more obvious than when we looked at the night sky. I saw supernovas and explosions, while she saw the stories behind these phenomena. I sought understanding, while she gave the stars meaning. Still... "Homecoming?" I replied. "I like that."

"It's no happily ever after," she said, "but it's enough."

Kyra grabbed my hands and twirled me, until I started laughing and we were so dizzy that the stars danced like fireflies.

Suddenly she stopped. I tripped over my own feet and skidded across the ice.

"It is enough," she repeated in a gasp as she tried to regain her breath. "It doesn't have to be a happily ever after or happily always. Just a happily once. A happily sometimes. Hope. That'd make our pain worth it." For a few seconds, she looked intensely sad. Then she curled her fingers around my hand. "Come on, we'll tell each other stories."

While we watched the stars in the sky, she wove tales of promise and heartbreak. Tales of Lost Creek itself.

As dawn settled around us, I felt Kyra slip away from me. Her smile faded. I clung to her. I hated these episodes. They scared me because I never knew what to expect from her.

In the end, she was the one who spoke up first.

"Rowanne thinks these new mood stabilizers aren't helping enough," she said quietly. She wove her fingers through her hair and tugged. "Again."

"I'm sorry." That was the best consolation I could offer. She'd tried most of the common treatments, but her manic episodes had become more intense. She went for weeks with minimal sleep. She spent days upon days drawing, painting, listening to tunes that only she could hear. At the same time, her depression had grown darker. Some days, she was so lost within herself that no one could reach her, no matter how much I wanted to lead her out. And both were happening more often.

"She thinks it might be better to try something new." Kyra picked up a stick and drew figures in the snow.

"She's been in touch with a treatment center in Fairbanks. She wants me to go. To try other medications under more supervision, more intense therapy."

"Oh." Plenty of people in Lost talked about sending Kyra to a residential treatment facility, but this was the first time she had spoken of it herself.

"It feels like defeat, you know?"

I bit my lip. "It isn't."

"I know, but it still feels like it is. I want medication that helps. I want my therapy sessions with Rowanne to be enough. I want my studies and my stories and our friendship to carry me through. I don't want to need anything more." She pulled her knees to her chest and hunched her shoulders forward.

"Do you want to go?" I asked. I didn't know what else to say.

She didn't look at me. "If you're leaving this summer... Without you here, I think it might be a good idea."

"Oh." I wanted her to be healthy, and I tried to support her—but I'd started to lose faith that Kyra could find a way back to a life between her extremes.

"Corey..." Her voice twisted in loneliness.

"I think it's a good idea too." I forced my voice to sound sincere. "It might help you. It might make you be better."

"You don't think I'm enough like this." She looked at me then, her eyes sad. Because for all we had shared—skinny dipping in the lake, reading horror stories in the deepest parts of the forest—her illness had increasingly been coming between us. She was trying to accept and live with her illness, and I was struggling to understand that.

"I think you could be so much more. I want to see you happy."

She seemed on the verge of responding, then thought better of it. She was quiet for a time, then asked, "Will you come back to me?"

"Always." I wrapped my arms around her. "Will you wait for me?"

She leaned into me. "Always."

POSTCARD FROM KYRA TO COREY
UNSENT

Your postcard arrived today, Cor. Where did you even find one? Mrs. Morden had to dig through the archives to find me this ancient postcard to write. *Greetings from Lost Creek Hot Springs, the fountain to cure all ills!* It's fitting, I guess.

Do you remember the first time we snuck out to the spa? Wondering what secrets it held? There are no secrets anymore, or maybe there are only secrets. And this is the one I hold closest: hearing from you gives me hope. Hope that I will see you again. Hope that I may get out of here.

But hope is the cruelest of all.

I miss you.

NOW HERE'S TO YOU

MRS. ROBINSON IS AS OLD AS THE STONES, AS OLD AS Lost Creek. When she sees me coming up the walk to her home at the edge of town, she opens her door. She wraps her hands around mine, at once stronger and frailer than I thought she would be. She barely reaches my shoulder now, but she's as fierce as an avalanche.

"Oh, Corey." She ushers me into her living room, overwhelming me with hospitality and questions about my life.

Once I've assured her I'm all right and my mother and brother are well, she pours me a cup of tea from the teapot already waiting on the coffee table. Mrs. Robinson is always prepared to have visitors.

"It's good to have you back. No matter what anyone else may say, the outside world isn't made for people like us. You belong here."

Her warmth wraps around me like a blanket. I *want* to belong here. "Lost is so different now that Kyra is gone."

"I miss her too, dear. Everyone does. It's sad to lose someone so young and talented."

"She had so many stories to tell," I say.

"And so much of her art to share."

"The paintings... Did you believe..." I struggle to find the words. It's absurd to ask her if she believes Kyra's paintings predicted the future. Or if she believes Kyra was the prophetess Piper seems to think she was.

Mrs. Robinson says, "Oh, I'm too old for the folly of the rest of the town."

"Is that what you think it is?" *Because I don't know what to think.*

Mrs. Robinson lifts her teacup and regards me over the rim. "Consider it a matter of perspective, then. I've spent decades in this town—lifetimes to some. I have seen it resist change, then embrace it countless times. I have seen it fight off financial problems when the mine closed and rise from the ashes. It's good fertilizer, ashes. If used sparingly and knowingly, ashes will help your garden grow."

Ashes. My tea suddenly tastes bitter. "Kyra *died*. How does her death help anyone?"

"Change isn't easy."

I'm not naive enough to think that nothing changes. I know that change can be uncomfortable. But it shouldn't *hurt*, not like this. "It's not right."

"I didn't say it was. But it's not the end of the world. Very little is, in fact, although we would like to pretend otherwise."

"Everything that happened at White Wolf Lake… It was the end of *Kyra's* world. Doesn't that count for something?"

Mrs. Robinson considers me. Her skin is thin like parchment, but her eyes are still sharp. Kyra always told me she couldn't imagine living to a hundred, but if she did, she wanted to be like Mrs. Robinson: graceful and surrounded by flowers.

"Come," Mrs. Robinson says. She grabs her cane and gets to her feet, with practiced ease. "Let me show you something."

PLANTING SEEDS

MRS. ROBINSON TAKES ME WITH SLOW DETERMINATION
through the house. We walk down the hall covered with sepia
photos from another lifetime. In the kitchen, which always
vaguely smells of rhubarb crumble, she stops at the back door.

I stare through the window, bewildered, as laughter floats
in from outside.

Mrs. Robinson's garden isn't winter ready. The plants
aren't protected against the snow. The furniture isn't covered.
And the little shed's door is open. It makes my fingers itch.
This garden doesn't only belong to Mrs. Robinson; we all
take ownership by helping her tend it. And preparing it for
winter is a communal task.

But.

On the other side of the fence, the snow is knee deep and continues to fall. Despite that, Mrs. Robinson's garden is in full bloom.

She comes to stand next to me, leaning heavily on her cane. "Close your mouth, dear. It's unbecoming."

My mouth snaps shut, but I can't stop staring. The garden is *alive*. One side is filled entirely with blooming salmonberry shrubs. A few of the younger teens—Gwen and Willow Wilde and Henry Lucas—mill about between the plants, picking ripe berries. Tobias Morden smiles and waves when he sees me.

I wave back. Any other time I would've walked over to talk to him, but my thoughts are going a hundred miles a minute. *What happened here? How can this garden be in bloom?*

The other half of the garden is covered in wildflowers. Yellow poppies run from the center path to the hedges, which frame the garden. It's a sea of flowers. Purple lupine borders the edges. The Harper brothers weed around the flowers, even though the ground should be hard and frozen.

The only snow sticking in the garden is the snow that clings to people's hair and boots. Otherwise it's spring. Summer. Berry season. *Life*.

"Kyra cared for this garden," Mrs. Robinson says.

"Once she moved to the spa, she spent less time here, but she'd still come every couple of days to tend the ground and the plants. On the days that she couldn't make it, Piper was here. Or young Tobias. Or Sam. Or any of the others. We wanted to make the garden winter ready, but Kyra was adamant that we shouldn't. I would sit with Kyra for hours then, even when the days began to shorten. She would paint without care for rest or food."

The bright colors of the flowers keep distracting me, and it takes a little while for Mrs. Robinson's words to register.

"I doubted her, at first. But then the garden started to grow. Flowers started to appear that hadn't been in this garden for years. The salmonberry shrubs started to bloom again. We had no explanation for it—*Kyra* had no explanation for it—but we couldn't deny what we saw in front of us." Mrs. Robinson takes my hand and walks me to the shed. Nothing is stored away. All the tools are still in use.

She points me around the side of the structure to the outer wall, which I couldn't see from the house. It's another painting of Kyra's, but one far more realistic than her usual style. It depicts a garden filled with salmonberries, purple lupine, and other wildflowers. It's a garden that mirrors Mrs. Robinson's garden almost exactly as it is looks now.

"The world doesn't end when one of us leaves it. We

change by being here. Kyra left behind a tangible legacy. She created art. She created this too. Do you understand?"

I open my mouth and close it again.

"Corey?" Mrs. Robinson's voice takes on an edge.

It's habit to say *yes, ma'am*. But instead, I clamp my mouth shut and shake my head.

I don't understand. And I don't think I ever will.

TO THOSE WE HAVE LOVED AND LOST

I CLOSE THE GARDEN GATE BEHIND ME AND WANDER back to the center of town, lost in thought. The garden looked so different back when Kyra and I kissed. Being with Kyra was easy, comfortable. The conversation that followed our kiss was anything but. I didn't want to remember it. I *don't* want to remember it.

But I can't ignore that memory.

"It's okay."

I start walking away from Mrs. Robinson's house.

"It's okay."

And I remember.

A YEAR AND A HALF BEFORE

WE FINISHED TENDING THE GARDEN IN SILENCE. THEN I waited outside while Kyra went in to say goodbye to Mrs. Robinson. After that, we walked to the woods at the edge of town, away from the houses, away from people. The only company we might have would be moose.

"It's okay," Kyra said, her back to me.

I put my hand on her shoulder.

"No, it's not," I said. "I want to be able to talk about this, about us."

"I just…" She raked her fingers through her hair before taking off her glasses to polish them, a sure sign she was nervous. "You shouldn't be apologizing to me. I'm sorry. I misread the signs."

"You didn't. Or maybe you did—but I did too."

She made a face. "I'm not *that* bad a kisser, am I?"

"No, you fool." I punched her lightly in the arm, but quickly sobered. "I kissed you because I was curious, because I wanted to know what all the fuss was about. I thought maybe if I tried it, I'd be…" I stumbled over the words, because the only way to understand my own feelings was to voice them, but I didn't want to hurt Kyra. While kissing may have been a one-time thing for me, it wasn't for her. "I'm not attracted to you. I don't think I've ever been attracted to anyone. That's not how it works for me."

"So it's not me, it's you?"

I grimaced. "Something like that. I love you, but I'm not in love with you."

"I love you, and I *am* in love with you," she said quietly.

"I know."

This time, when Kyra turned away from me, I let her be.

Her shoulders tensed and her knuckles turned white from gripping her own arms so tightly. Even if she didn't want me to see her cry, I couldn't ignore how silent sobs racked her body. But all I could do was simply be there, close to her—and wait.

After some time, she calmed and spoke. "I don't want to lose you." I'd never heard her sound so fragile before.

"I don't want to lose you either," I whispered. Friendship was all I could give her, and I wasn't sure it was enough.

"You're all I have in this town. I don't want to push you away."

I stepped close and wrapped my arms around her. She felt as taut as a bear trap. "I won't let you push me away."

"Promise?"

I stood on tiptoe and pressed a kiss into her hair. "You're my best friend. I love you endless days and endless nights. You're stuck with me."

She sighed and some of the tension eased from her shoulders. "I would be utterly lost without you."

PHONE CALL

"Is Mom there, Luke?"

"She's at a meeting at the hospital. You know how it goes. She won't be home for another couple of hours. Why, what do you need?"

"I..."

"Corey? Is something wrong?"

"I..."

"Cor?"

"Sorry, I forgot how terrible the reception is here."

"Yeahhh. Tell me about something I do miss."

"Like grizzlies?"

"They're hibernating."

"Eagles?"

"Migratory."

"Mrs. Robinson's rhubarb crumble."

"It's not the season for rhubarb, Corey. You know that."

"Mrs. H's cookies."

"No fair. I do miss those. I'll get on the next plane to Lost."

"I'll be—I'd be home by the time you got here."

"Corey? Are you sure you're okay? You sound weird. Weirder than normal."

"Shut up, punk. It's… It's strange to be back here, you know? I thought everything would be the same, but so much has changed. Did you know they're even talking about reopening the mine? I thought Lost would always be home, but I'm not sure where home is anymore."

"Home is still there. And school.

And here, with Mom and me. As long as you don't take the train straight back to school without coming to see us. The new house really isn't that bad. Mom finally decorated the living room."

"I want to be here to say goodbye. Then I'm flying to Fairbanks, then home to see you. Okay?"

"Better."

"You are a punk."

"I try. Hey, Corey? I liked Kyra too. She was nice to me. She was your best friend. It's okay if you're not okay."

"Hey, Luke?"

"Yeah?"

"Are you and Mom okay?"

"Are you sure you don't want to call Mom's cell phone?"

"No, no. Don't worry about it. I don't want to—"

"Everything is all right here, I promise. Mom and I are okay."

"Thanks."

"Cor?"

"Yes?"

"Will you say hi to Tobias for me?

And Sam? And will you bring home some of Mrs. Henderson's cookies? Tell her I miss them, and tell her I miss her too. And that I'm sorry about Kyra."

"I will, I promise. See you soon."

"Hey, sis?"

"Yeah?"

"Don't freeze your toes off out there."

PATHWAYS

I DON'T CONSCIOUSLY THINK ABOUT WHERE I WANT TO go, my feet just take me. I head toward the workers' residences that were built after the gold rush, when quartz mining took off. This is the shabby part of town. Unlike the houses on Main, these houses are small and creaky, with roofs that groan under the weight of snow. But even though the walls could barely keep the cold out, they kept the warmth in.

Home.

Before Dad left, we were four against the world. After that, Mom traveled back and forth between Lost and Fairbanks and the surrounding towns more and more, and

Luke and I fended for ourselves, with the help of neighbors, especially Sheriff Flynn, the Hendersons, and the Mordens. Kyra would come over to play board games with the two of us until long past midnight. Luke, Tobias, and I would play ball in the yard. Seven months ago, I was at home here.

Luke's Lost Creek is the town I remember. Every year, Lost would bond over the Yukon Quest dogsled race. We'd celebrate the new year with large bonfires. And we would eat the most absurd meals when the ice prevented supplies from coming in and Jan's grocery store from being stocked.

Once you've settled in, you should walk over, Piper told me yesterday.

I turn the corner and search my pocket for a key I no longer own, for a place that is no longer mine, and I come to a dead stop.

Because at the end of the street, there is no house. Support beams stand, singed and blackened. Parts of the roof lie half buried under the snow. A magenta ribbon is tied to the remains of the gate. The house that I once called home is gone.

On what used to be our threshold, a handful of pink flowers peek out of a drift of snow. I brush away the snow and stare at the frozen salmonberry blossoms. They're crumbled and torn. A message is scrawled on one of the support beams.

Three simple words: *So be it.*

Mrs. Robinson's voice echoes in my ears. *It's good fertilizer, ashes. If used sparingly and knowingly, ashes will help your garden grow.*

ABANDON HOPE

NINE MONTHS BEFORE

I NIBBLED ON MY PEN CAP AND STARED AT GLOW-IN-THE-dark stars that I'd carefully placed on my ceiling. Kyra and I were both working on assignments for one of the remote English classes all the juniors and seniors took. Which was to say, she was working while I was waiting for inspiration. I would take math over literature any day.

"'Through me you must go into the city of sorrow: through me you must go into eternal pain: through me you must go among the lost people,'" Kyra read, then scribbled something in her notebook. "'Abandon all hope, you who enter here.'" She looked up. "Does that not sound like Lost to you?"

"Dante's inscription over the gate of Hell?" I laughed. "No, not particularly. It sounds depressing."

Her eyes flashed. "Is that what you think my depressive episodes are like? Eternal pain?"

"I—I didn't mean—" I stammered. "I didn't mean it like that. It's a turn of phrase. I don't know what your episodes are like." I'd thought about asking her but never actually did. I could never find the right words. Mostly because, to me, her depressions were synonymous with closed doors and loneliness, and they scared me. I didn't know how to fix them for her.

Kyra wet her lips. "I was reading through Grandfather's history of Lost last night. 'As the story goes, the town of Lost Creek, Alaska, isn't named after the eponymous stream. It's named after its first group of colonial settlers, a handful of adventurers, for whom the world didn't have a place anymore. Lost men, who didn't belong anywhere else.'" The cadence of Kyra's voice lends weight to her words. "'They set down their roots, stealing land that was never theirs, and carved their home between the mountains and the mines, the hot springs, the river, and the lake, during those long summer days when anything seemed possible. Then the cold came. And these settlers discovered that they had built their home in the heart of winter. They'd come for new opportunity, but they found that winter is not malleable, and frost settles too. And no matter how hard they tried, they could not escape being lost.'"

I shivered in delight.

Kyra didn't smile. "Or maybe it said, 'They could not escape Lost.' Grandfather's handwriting is hard to decipher sometimes."

I gazed out of my window, to the front yard where Luke and Tobias were playing ball. "That's quite a difference."

"No." Kyra shook her head and picked up her pen again. "It really isn't."

GIFTS

I START AWAKE IN THE MIDDLE OF THE NIGHT. THE lights are still on—I didn't want to be surrounded by darkness. My thoughts and dreams are dark enough. The outbuilding is quiet. Everything is still. I'd locked the closet and pushed the desk chair against it. But my heart is hammering out of control.

I don't know what woke me. Despite the room being silent, I do not feel alone. I can feel eyes on me. I can hear the soft sound of breathing. But I don't turn to my side or look around because I know if I do, I'll find another presence in this room, someone leaning against the desk.

Kyra used to do this. She'd sit and watch me. And when she got restless, she'd jump on my bed in the middle of the night, scaring the life out of me. I wait for the covers to move, for the bed to creak under her weight.

They don't. But the feeling of being watched doesn't abate. It grows stronger. A chill runs along my spine.

I close my eyes, shift my head, and force myself to look into the room. *No one.*

Then my gaze travels over to my backpack. I'd dumped my clothes in a hasty pile on top of it before I went to sleep. It had toppled over to lean against the desk.

A handful of freshly picked salmonberry flowers rest on my shirt.

I grow cold despite the heavy blankets I'm burrowed in. I push the covers aside and walk over to the backpack. The floor is ice under my feet.

When I brush the flowers away, the hair on the back of my neck stands on end.

Tucked into my shirt lies a pencil sketch of me, a scene like the one from the airstrip yesterday. My backpack is slung over my shoulder. In the distance stands a girl who may be Piper. Who may be Kyra.

Come to me.

DAY THREE

WHOLESOME LIVES
AND HOT SPRINGS

Kyra was here. She was here, and she's waiting for me. I can't shake the thought from my mind. *She's still waiting for me.*

I have to go to her.

After breakfast, I tell Mrs. Henderson I'm going to take a walk. I don't tell that her I'm going to the spa, in case she tries to stop me. But before I can go to the memorial this afternoon, I need to know where she lived—*how* she lived—as well as how she died.

With my lunch packed, I make the trek to the hot springs. Although a solitary road leads from Lost Creek to the spa, it's overgrown and doesn't get plowed in winter, so I follow the shortcut through the woods.

In the early morning twilight, it's an easy walk, more so than in the afternoon when the branches cast shadows and the trees whisper. It isn't snowing, which is a rare occurrence in winter, and I'm going to see Kyra.

Part of me knows it's not rational, expecting to find her at the hot springs, but that doesn't stop my heart from racing. I'm giddy with hope. I envelop myself in the wild beauty of our nature. The pine forest seems to go on forever. In spring, it's not only humans who inhabit these parts, but bears and moose and eagles. Many a summer, we've had black bears stroll down Main, and if a moose tried to eat its way through Mrs. Robinson's garden, it wouldn't be the first time. It's a coexistence that's as natural as breathing.

Yet, in winter, it's quieter. And even though the bears hibernate and the eagles migrate, the land is still beautiful. The vast layer of snow tucks us in, softening color and sound. I've always thought we don't need a church in Lost because we have nature to inspire awe.

Gradually, the hot springs come into view, as does the spa. It's an old, burgundy hotel with two floors, sloped roofs, and rooms for maybe two dozen guests. According to Kyra, it was built at the start of the twentieth century. The hot springs were first used by miners on their way to or from the Klondike. But in the following decades, it became an increasingly popular tourist destination. Although Lost Creek couldn't compete with the hot springs in Circle or Chena, it had a steady clientele for almost half a century. Now that it's abandoned, we've made it ours. Kyra and me. And before us, Anna. Amy. Will. Those of us who've escaped Lost over the years have all carved our names in the banister, leaving a piece of ourselves behind.

I slow down. Kyra and I always snuck in through the back because, technically, we weren't supposed to be there. The building was considered by the town to be a monument to its history and therefore out of bounds for us. But if Lost knew that Kyra was staying here, then presumably the front door would be unbolted and unlocked?

I pause and eye the road leading up to the spa.

I could ask Aaron, the groundskeeper, who lives not far from here in a small, modern cabin. Or I could simply try the door. But neither option feels right. Kyra wants me here.

So I stick to the tree line as I circle the hotel, to sneak in like old times.

....

I haul myself in through a small window on the north side of the building and end up on what Kyra and I had deduced must have once been a kitchen counter. The room itself is yellowed and empty. The floor around the counter is caked in mud. A little snow has blown in.

I jump down and stamp the snow off my boots. Mine aren't the only prints here. I crouch and my heart hammers. The others are dry and at least a few days old. It's hard to tell the size of the boots—the prints aren't clear enough—but I convince myself they're Kyra's. I want them to be hers. I trace the prints, imaging her climbing in through this window on one of her adventures. I imagine her alive and well.

Kyra.

I follow the tracks to the hallway that runs along the back of the building, through the service quarters. One door leads directly from this hallway to the entrance, but it's locked and the lock has long since rusted shut. So instead, I follow the footprints up a narrow staircase to the second floor. It's convoluted and damp, but a small price to pay for a private hideout. Besides, Kyra and I walked these steps so many times, I could navigate this place from muscle memory.

The walls here are covered in faded graffiti. In old photos, this place looked resplendent, with thick carmine carpet and gold-threaded wallpaper, but those days passed long ago.

I head toward the foyer, staying away from the creaky

wooden bannister. Leaning on it too hard could send it, and me, spiraling down to the first floor. Instead, I stand at the top of the stairs like a fairy-tale princess in a parka and jeans. And I stare.

The entrance is a large space that is open to the second floor, and it has become a riot of colors. It's filled with flowers and paintings and candles and papers. It's as bright as it ever was dusty, and it looks far more alive than the rest of the building.

In front of the fireplace, which bears traces of recent use, are two comfortable-looking chairs. A few sketchbooks are stacked on the side table.

I slowly descend the stairs, and with every step I take, I notice more details.

On the far side of the room, on a large table, is a collection of sketches and sketchbooks and paints and other art supplies. Candles and melted wax are clustered in front of paintings and drawings that are propped up against the walls. The flower bouquets around them are withered, but I see salmonberry flowers and little specks of magenta everywhere I turn.

This isn't a hangout or a home. It's a shrine.

BIRDS WITH BROKEN WINGS

SEVEN MONTHS BEFORE

In a place like Lost Creek, our entire world was a handful of square miles, bordered by water, trees, and mountains. But when Kyra was painting, she forgot the confines of Lost, of realism. Painting stilled the constant churning of her mind. It gave her an outlet, though she hardly ever remembered it afterward.

It was either painting or running through the forest, she told me, and when she was painting, she couldn't trip over roots or fall down a hill. It was self-care, she said. She needed to escape her mania one way or another.

It was June, and Kyra let me watch. She didn't usually tolerate observers, but it was the week before Mom, Luke, and I would be leaving for Winnipeg and Mom's new job at the children's hospital. We had so little time left together, and neither of us wanted to spend time apart.

We sat on the dock at White Wolf Lake, and she had a large sketchbook in front of her. I held her paints, although I wasn't sure if she noticed I was there. She was working so fervently, and I kept holding my breath, as if I were watching an athletic race.

Despite the fact she used limited colors and shades that were more vivid than the scenery around us, it didn't take me long to recognize her subject matter.

Luke was the first to appear on the page. His eyes were a smidge too green and bright, his hair too spiky, but it was him. I'd never seen Kyra draw him like that, and something in the way she made him smile punched me right in the chest. She was so talented. And he looked so happy.

She depicted him in motion, running toward us. It looked as though he could step out of the page at any moment.

Next, Tobias. Piper's brother. Of course they'd be together. The two of them always were. In her painting, he followed behind Luke at some distance, holding something in his hand. As Kyra continued, the details became clearer and clearer. From Tobias's hoodie to the boots he wore to the bird he held in his palm. A kestrel—in bright magenta—with one wing at an awkward angle.

It was the perfect Lost Creek scene.

Kyra continued adding trees and shadows behind the two boys, adding depth and distance. From what little I'd seen of Kyra's art, she preferred to paint the flowers of Mrs. Robinson's garden or draw landscapes of places far beyond our hometown, into the realm of imagination. This was the first time I could think of that Kyra had painted someone from Lost Creek.

She kept going for a while longer, adding nuance and improving on flaws I didn't see. And she kept messing with the image. She changed colors near the edges. She turned half of the forest blue. All the while, I was mesmerized by her brushwork.

Then her hands started to tremble, and she swayed on the dock.

She put down her brush. If she could've gone on, it wouldn't have surprised me if she'd changed the boys' clothes or their expressions.

"It's beautiful," I said softly.

She glanced at me and then at the painting, then she looked away. "Eh."

Her gaze darted across the horizon, as if the restlessness were building inside her again. These episodes always made her look haunted, and I longed to be the one to anchor her.

She started to close her sketchbook when I snatched it from her. "Wait a minute. Let it dry."

"Why?"

I shook my head. "Luke would love how you portrayed him and Tobias with that bird—like heroes."

Her smile was crooked. Forced. "We could all do with more heroes." She climbed to her feet, stretched, and began to pace.

"We could always do with more heroes," I agreed as I stared at the painting. She'd lost herself in the act of creating before, but I'd never seen her produce work like this. Even with a limited color palate, this looked *real*.

Yet she didn't see how impressive it was.

"When you're in Canada," she said, still pacing, "think of me?"

I looked up at her. "Do you honestly believe that I could forget you?"

Before she could answer, footsteps sounded on the dock behind us, and someone gasped. I turned to find Piper, staring at Kyra's painting. "That is magical."

Kyra shook her head but didn't say anything.

I didn't think Piper meant it literally. Maybe she did.

But the next Sunday, when Luke and Tobias went hiking in the woods, they returned carrying a kestrel with a broken wing. Tobias held the bird in his hands, while Luke ran ahead to find a box and call the wildlife center.

Kyra had all but forgotten about the painting. She'd gone through countless sketches and paintings since that one, and afterward, she tore them all up. But I'd liberated this painting from her sketchbook before she got to it. It was neatly pressed between my schoolbooks at home. I hadn't forgotten it.

And by the way Piper stared at us the next time we went into town, neither had she.

A SHRINE OF BLOSSOMS

I PAUSE AT THE BOTTOM OF THE STAIRS AND REACH FOR
the closest petals. The flowers that appeared in my
bedroom were soft, almost like silk. These petals crumble
between my fingers.

It's like this place is suspended in time, untouched
since Kyra left it, or perhaps longer than that. It seems
so fragile that a whisper could bring it down. It's not a
chapel, but a house of cards.

I touch one of the ribbons the same way Piper did
when I first arrived. Reverently.

On the mantel, there are more salmonberry blossoms
in different shapes and forms. Some are dried flowers,

others are painted onto the marble, even crocheted from yarn. A small brown bottle with a cork sits among the flowers. Salmonberry perfume? I don't smell it. It's hard enough to breathe.

Scattered between the flowers—real flowers, fake flowers—lie bits of burned paper. Some still bear the faint traces of words. *Please. I implore you. Help me.* None of them are in Kyra's handwriting.

It's as if the distorted focus of these last two days shifts—and clears.

She foresaw. She foretold.

Lost didn't just assign meaning to Kyra's paintings, they made requests of her. They placed her in this house of pilgrimage and, by the looks of all the offerings, revered her.

We found meaning together, Sheriff Flynn told me. I'd assumed he meant Kyra and the town had found a way to understand each other. But now I can't help but wonder if he meant the town had found a purpose for Kyra, a meaning for the girl they'd decided was meaningless after she was diagnosed.

Corey?

I turn toward the whisper, but the room is empty. All I can hear is the pounding of my own heart.

I walk toward the large table and carefully open one of the sketchbooks. A saucer with dried ink stands next to it. Neither disappear when I touch them, although it wouldn't have surprised me if they had. This place seems enchanted.

The sketchbook is filled with inked drawings. In fact, all the sketchbooks are. They're rougher and courser than Kyra's paintings, with haphazard colors and harsh pen strokes. Flowers. Mountains. Faces. Some I recognize, some I don't. The spa. The hot springs. White Wolf Lake, this time—thank goodness—without Kyra in it.

When I flip to the final page of one of the sketchbooks, I pause. The drawing is coarse, the ink blotched. But I recognize myself, and the charred skeleton of my house in front of me. The scene is exactly as it was last night, as if she had been present to observe me.

We bonded over art.

I've only been gone for seven months, and Kyra only used to paint to burn off the energy of her manic episodes. But judging by the evidence around town, Kyra had painted enough to last a lifetime.

No star can burn forever, they said.

Kyra burned so brightly. Until she had nothing left to give.

I'm surrounded by countless paintings, but where are Kyra's books? Her stories? Her studies?

The only words here are questions, pleas.

And whispers.

Corey?

KEEPER OF THE SPA

AARON STANDS IN THE DOORWAY. ALTHOUGH HE'S OVER seventy years old, he's a tall, imposing man who worked in one of Mr. H's mines before the town asked him to become keeper of the spa, to mind the monumental building, to keep the wildlife out and the hot springs clean. His hair and skin have gone gray, but his arms and shoulders are still broad, and he always appears to squint in the light.

"Corey? Are you okay?"

I don't know what to say. I sit down at the bottom of the stairs. There's so much to take in. More flowers. More notes—or are they prayers?—from visitors. Black ribbons woven through the banister and the balustrade.

I gesture around me. "I wanted to see where Kyra had been living. But this... All of this..."

Aaron's gaze strays behind me. His mouth sets. "It's overwhelming, isn't it? The last few days, people have been visiting to pay their respects and to remember her."

"And before that? This is from more than a few days."

He nods. "Before that too."

A thousand questions tumble through my mind. *How long did Kyra live here? Was she on her own? Why was she here and not in Fairbanks? Why didn't she get help?* "What happened?"

Aaron's gaze strays past my shoulder again, as if someone were there, observing our conversation. It's unnerving. He shakes his head as he comes over and sits down on the step next to me, elbows on knees. "Kyra was a good girl," he says. "She should've had a long life ahead of her. But no one in Lost wished her any harm."

I want to object, but he shakes his head.

"I know it wasn't always like that, kid." His grimace softens to a smile. "Lost and Kyra learned to understand each other. They came to her, and they came to care for her too. I wish you'd been here to see it."

"They came to her with prayers and requests? She was bipolar, not a prophet."

My throat burns and my hands clench, wanting to hit something. I laugh because it's the only thing I can do. Kyra once told me about Sága, a protector in Norse mythology. A storyteller. A seeress. A goddess.

My voice is tight when I say, "*What did you all turn Kyra into?* A miracle? An oracle? What do you want to call her?"

He shakes his head at my outburst. "I'm not comfortable with those titles. But whether it was through art or observations, she brought wonder to Lost Creek. And with it, a future. Can you imagine? She painted a bright, prosperous town and the next thing we know, investors show up. This town has struggled against the elements for so long, but now it has hope again. Kyra brought that future to us. She changed us."

I blink. I try to wrap my mind around his words. "How?"

"She saw a future that none of us could see yet. She *believed* in a future, and for that, we believed in her."

Four words, but they carry the weight of lifetimes. *We believed in her.*

"She was a bright star, and she burned herself out. All we have left is the truth, and maybe that's nothing more than a story too." He shakes his head. "You know how much she liked stories."

I laugh again, and it comes out bitter and broken. This room is too small. The air is too stale. Kyra's art is everywhere, but none of her books. "This wasn't her story."

"Sorry?"

I shake my head. "Did she like being here?" I ask. "Was it her choice?"

Aaron gets to his feet and brushes off his pants. Again, he glances behind me, and he hesitates before giving me a forced smile. "Of course she did. She belonged here."

WRITING ON THE WALL

AARON DOESN'T WANT TO LEAVE ME ON MY OWN, BUT
when I tell him I need a moment to myself, he gives me
that time. I grab the drawings Kyra made of me and stuff
them in my pocket.

Lost Creek is full of stories too, Kyra had said.
*Stories of love and secrets. Of friendship and survival.
Of hate.*

I can't breathe. I want to scream. I want to claw
through my skin.

And I need to get out, out, *out*. Away from this shrine.
Three steps at a time, I bound up the stairs. Outside, a
storm cloud must pass by, because the little sunlight that

filters in through the windows disappears. I'm suddenly surrounded by shadows.

When light seeps in again, it's different, dimmer.

I sink against the wall and wrap my arms around my knees because it's the only way I can keep from shaking. I catch my breath. The second floor is grayer, the air is colder, and I gulp.

What did they do to her?

What did they do *to her?*

What did we *do to her?*

I can't stop trembling, but I need to find more signs of Kyra's life here.

But the second floor, which consists primarily of bedrooms that were used when the spa was still a tourist attraction, is mostly empty. Aside from a few footsteps in the dust, it's largely untouched. I zigzag my way through the two wings of the building, until I reach the last room in the east wing.

The door stands slightly ajar, and inside, I see a flash of color.

A bright blue sleeping bag sits on top of an old bed. A portable radiator stands at the foot of the bed, and at the head is a bedside table with a lamp and a book on it.

The book is in my hands and clutched to my chest before I'm aware of what I'm doing.

Oral Tradition and Storytelling in the Arctic. Kyra

read this book until it started to fall apart. I almost laugh out loud. *Nerd*. My loveable, weird best friend. This was the Kyra I knew.

I sit on the bed, and my vision blurs. *She was here.*

The room wouldn't be remarkable but for the fact Kyra stayed here. The bedside lamp switches on and off—apparently Aaron fixed the generator. A bundle of purple cloth lies next to the pillow. I pick it up and unfold it. It's a scarf with subtle threads of silver and tiny stars sewn onto it. They follow constellations. The Big Dipper. Cassiopeia. Cygnus—the swan. Lyra. Orion. The stars we saw together.

I gave this scarf to Kyra for her seventeenth birthday, almost a year ago. When Mom accepted her new job, Kyra held me close, wrapped the scarf around us, and reminded me we'd still be under the same night sky.

I bring the scarf to my face and inhale. There is no trace of her. My hands thump back into my lap as I take in the rest of the room.

The walls are covered with writing. It's the same phrase, repeated over and over again.

I can't breathe. I can't breathe. I can't breathe. I can't breathe. I can't breathe.

Now nothing can stop my shaking. I stand, clinging tightly to the scarf, and move from one wall to the other.

I can't stay.

It's everywhere, on all the walls. Scrawled in pencil and pen, in blue and black and the bloodiest red. All in Kyra's distinctive script.

Then above the door:

They're watching. The shadows, Corey. They're always watching.

I want to reach up and trace my name, but it's too high. Higher still, in the farthest corner, more scribbles:

Don't go.

NIGHTMARES

EIGHT MONTHS BEFORE

WE SPENT LENGTHENING EARLY SUMMER NIGHTS AT THE
spa, when it was still light enough for Kyra and me to
walk home, no matter the hour. We lay on the roof, staring
up at the midnight sun, shoulder to shoulder.

"I hate summer," Kyra said. "The light goes on forever,
and my thoughts won't stop. I can't breathe here."

I threaded my fingers through hers. "Winter will come
soon, and the nights will be darker again."

"Not soon enough." She sighed. "Besides, you're
scared of the dark."

"I don't like shadows. I don't like not being able to see. I am *not* scared of the dark."

She smiled. "Liar. You're terrified of night, which seems rather irrational for an aspiring astronomer. But I'll stand beside you. I'll face the shadows with you."

"I'm not scared," I lied. But I was. Scared of the darkness, of the nights, ever since Dad left. Scared of waking up in the morning to discover another part of our family missing.

"It's okay if you are." She muttered something else but so quietly that I couldn't hear it. I could guess though. I was terrified of her nights too.

I clung to her hand. "What if we can't build a life outside of Lost, even with Mom's new job?"

She smiled. "You can always come back to me." With her free hand, she brushed a twig out of my hair. "I'm scared too."

I shifted so I could look at her.

She didn't speak for the longest time. "It scares me to think that my episodes will overtake me, that I'll lose myself completely. It scares me to think that one day, I'll see myself the way Lost sees me. That I won't be enough."

I hesitated and in that moment, Kyra tried to pull away from me. I held on tight. Kyra was always so full of life and wonder that I couldn't imagine her losing that. I didn't want to. "If that ever happens, I'll come back for you. I'll stand beside you. I'll face the shadows with you," I said. "But you'll tell me, won't you?"

She squeezed my hand, her thumb rubbing my palm. "I will always tell you everything. I promise."

I leaned back against the shingles. "You matter, Kyr. To me. To your family. To Lost, even if they don't always understand you."

"Then why don't I feel like I'm enough? Why does trying to fit in hurt so much? I can't always be there for you, and it feels like I keep disappointing you—keep scaring you away."

"You don't. Don't even think that." I blinked back tears I didn't want her to see, but I couldn't keep them from my voice. I propped myself up on one elbow. "We'll always be here for each other. And you should never settle for enough."

She buried her head against my shoulder, and in that embrace I could feel all of her pain. I held her. She shivered, and I cradled her closer. Kyra's sorrow left me empty, and I didn't know how to relieve it. But together we held our darkness up to the light, and it became easier to carry because we were not alone.

THE WAY THE
WORLD CHANGES

I SPENT MORE TIME AT THE SPA THAN I'D ANTICIPATED, and the sun has reached its highest point in the sky when I start back to town. Two lone figures walk back from the lake. I recognize Piper's silhouette, but I can't tell who the other person is until he looks up, and I see that it's Sam. Sam Flynn. The boy who never spoke and never smiled is now trading gibes and grinning at Piper.

Piper laughs.

Then Sam spots me. He points and says something, but I look away before Piper responds. I keep my head down as I walk back to Main. I pass two young girls having a snowball fight in their yard. Their squeals sound out of place, but they draw a smile from me nonetheless. It's the first time I've heard children laugh since I arrived.

"Corey!" Piper calls from behind me.

I stuff my hands deep into my pockets and pretend I don't hear. I don't want to deal with her hypocrisy right now.

But this is one of the downsides of a town the size of Lost; everyone can find anyone here if they want to. I used to think that was an upside. I felt like it was impossible to feel lost here—or to lose yourself.

"Corey." Piper's voice sounds a lot closer now, and I can't avoid her any longer.

I stop, but I don't turn.

She catches up with me and drags me to a corner, away from the road. She's pale and the circles under her eyes are dark. "How are you?"

I've had enough. I can't play this game anymore. "I went to the spa."

"And did you get the answers you were looking for?" she asks, although I'm quite sure she already knows.

"None at all."

Piper shakes her head and lets go of my arm. She looks genuinely disappointed, but she doesn't hold back. "You come barging in to investigate a murder that never happened. You come to tell us all that we did wrong when you weren't even here. You don't understand how much Kyra meant to this town."

"Is that why you kept her locked away in a ruined building? An artist, whose only job it was to produce? Did her meaning come from serving as Lost's own private oracle? Or did you actually see her as a member of this community?"

"Her art *mattered*."

"Her *art* was hardly the most important thing about her. She didn't even care about it."

"She loved her life in Lost Creek."

"And when she started painting her own death, you all didn't mind fulfilling her prophecies?"

Piper stills. "Kyra held this town together with her art. She was the example by which we took our inspiration—in her life, but also in her death. Kyra would've told you that the most important part of any story is the way it ends. We will remember her."

"Her death was an *inspiration*?"

Piper narrows her eyes. "That's an ugly way of putting it."

"It's an ugly sentiment."

"She pulled Lost together."

"And she shouldn't have had to die to do so."

If there's such a thing as a townwide, collective intake of breath, this may be it. Outside the post office, Mrs. Morden and old Mr. Wilde turn and stare. From a distance, Sam does too. Every single person out on the street stops, turns, stares.

Piper laughs. "Be careful, Corey. You still don't understand."

DO YOU UNDERSTAND NOW?

EXT. LOST—MAIN—AFTERNOON

....

*Corey continues toward the Hendersons'
house. She fumbles with her phone. Piper
and Sam walk away, but everyone else in
her path remains, frozen like set pieces.*

*Two young girls stand in the middle
of their yard. Each holds a snowball,
but they do not play.*

Girl #1:

Do you understand now?

Girl #2

Let me tell you a story.

Tobias Morden leans against a wall.

Tobias

Do you understand now, Corey?

Mrs. Morden

Let me tell you a story.

Corey ducks her head and refuses to acknowledge anyone. She picks up her pace. She doesn't see Roshan, who trails behind her, keeping an eye on all the townspeople.

Roshan

Do you understand?

Through the windows of every house that Corey passes, she sees Kyra's artwork. Simple paintings of families gathered together, of refurbished homes, of travel and riches. Paintings of carefully constructed happiness.

PHONE CALL

"Do you think it was more than suicide?"

"I really don't know, E. They turned her into an icon. They forgot that she was a person. They believed in a lie, but I never thought that was enough to kill someone."

"No?"

"What do you mean?"

"In my experience, words and beliefs kill people all the time."

"Oh. I never thought—"

"You never needed to."

"I'm sorry."

"Are you okay?"

"No. It hurts to be here, E. I miss her. I keep waiting for her to run around the corner and tell me that she was hiding. Everything feels wrong."

"That's not just because of Kyra. You don't feel at home anymore."

"I should."

"Lost changed. You changed."

"I didn't want it to. I didn't want to."

"Didn't you? You like life at St. James."

"But I always thought that Lost would still be home. If this isn't my home, then where is? Lost was everything I ever knew, but they look at me like I'm a trespasser. Like I don't matter anymore."

"You're at home here. You matter to us."

"It's not the same though."

"I know."

FEAR HER

I SLIP INTO MRS. H'S BAKERY AN HOUR BEFORE THE memorial. She's preparing food and she's still, as she called it the day I arrived, grief baking. When she sees me, she rushes toward the door. The pain in her eyes is as visible as the relief. She's gone pale. She grabs my arms as though I might otherwise disappear. "*Corey.* You left hours ago. We didn't know where you'd gone."

Those few words are enough to make me feel small and selfish.

"I'm sorry, Mrs. H, I—" I stop myself. What can I tell her? "I went to the spa and lost track of time."

"I should be used to that, shouldn't I? The two of you always did."

"I'm sorry," I repeat. "I didn't mean to scare you."

She shakes her head, and I wait for her to say more. To acknowledge why she's worried, or how Kyra simply walked out of our lives and she keeps waiting for her to come back too.

Instead, Mrs. H returns to her dough. She kneads with determination, but her methodic pounding doesn't mask the way her shoulders shake. Or the way tears drip from her cheeks, one at a time.

The bakery smells of yeast, cinnamon, and sugar. The heat from the ovens makes the space cozy. But it's not comfortable. *Comfort* implies an ease I don't feel. I'm stifled—and I want to get out. I want to leave Lost after the memorial.

Most of the bakery is used for actual baking, and Mrs. H has an impressive workspace that's open to the front. A few stools stand at the counter, for those visitors who drop by for a baked good and coffee and want to stay. I grab one. I hook my feet around the legs and balance on the edge of the seat.

"Mrs. H?" My voice sounds small, even to my ears, and maybe she picks up on it. She sets the dough aside and meets my gaze. "Mrs. H, I've seen the garden. I've seen the paintings."

"Oh."

I want to ask, *How could you let this happen?* What I ask instead is, "What happened?"

"It's a long story."

"I'm here to listen."

She pauses, and I can see that she's weighing how much to tell me. I want the truth, but apparently, that's not a simple request.

"Fear," she says, eventually. "The people of Lost Creek were afraid of Kyra because she was so different. I can't tell you how much that *hurt*. Especially because, at times, I was afraid of her myself. I didn't always understand her, but I wanted her to be happy." She shakes her head when I start to interrupt. "I only began to understand Kyra when I began to understand her art. She painted that."

Mrs. H points to a small canvas of Kyra and her sitting on a rickety bench outside the hot springs. The spa was our special place, but I knew that Kyra wanted to share the hot springs with her parents. She wanted to tell them about her stories. She wanted to talk them into letting her travel and go to college.

In the painting, Kyra shows her mother a book. The two of them are surrounded by salmonberry flowers.

"The same held true for most everyone in Lost Creek. Once they understood—"

"She was a person with hopes and dreams." Try as I might, I can't keep the anger out of my voice.

"She helped the community, and they learned to stop fearing her. She was different, yes, but we finally understood that that was *good*. Until then, we hadn't understood that we could help her too, better than any outsider could."

"Rowanne? She was a *therapist*. Kyra needed therapy and medication."

"Even when they didn't work?" Mrs. H counters. Kyra struggled with medication from the time she first got her diagnosis. She responded to drugs, but marginally. They dimmed her mania for a while, but it would only come back stronger. "She was my daughter. All I *wanted* was for the therapy and medication to work. It broke my heart when they didn't. It was only then that Joe realized—that *we* realized—that we'd been wrong all along."

"But when I left—"

"We tried everything," Mrs. H interrupts me quietly. "I wish you would believe me."

When I left, Kyra was talking about therapy regimens. Other options. When I left, she still had *hope*. But if the state of the spa is anything to go by, at the end, she had nothing left but her paintings to draw out her restless energy.

It takes me a moment to register Mrs. H's earlier words. "What do you mean you'd been wrong?"

"All of the medications she'd tried only suppressed her creativity."

I blink. Something clicks.

Kyra never mentioned that. And Rowanne would never have left of her own volition. And the depths of Kyra's mania... I push off the stool and it clatters to the floor. "You withheld her medication?"

"We didn't give up without a fight." I turn to find Mr. H standing in the doorway. He clings to his briefcase like a lifeline, his shoulders still sagging. "The medication didn't work, Corey," he says. "You know that. She would feel better for brief increments of time, but she'd inevitably get worse again. It was cruel to make her go through those ups and downs."

I ball my fists and I honest-to-God see *red*. "But the medication *did* work. Maybe not perfectly. Maybe not as much as she wanted it to, but she wanted to keep exploring other options. And between the medication and her sessions with Rowanne, she wanted to be *better*."

"She couldn't paint," Mr. H says.

"She didn't want to!" Kyra wasn't *happy* when she was painting. She was *coping*.

"But *we* did," he says softly. He walks over to Mrs. H, who keeps her head down. "You don't understand, Corey. We needed the light that she brought."

His words join the refrain of Lost Creek. *You don't belong here. Outsider. Stranger.*

I want to pound the wall in frustration. "She was deeply unhappy."

Mr. H merely shakes his head. "There's no way for you to know that. We understood our daughter. We did what was best for her, and for all of us."

"You didn't understand her. You didn't listen to her. And you aren't listening to me now." I'm not sure how much of this I think and how much of it I actually speak aloud, but Mr. H blanches.

I take a step back, but he pulls himself together. "The memorial is starting soon. Make sure you're ready. We will remember her the way she deserved—with respect."

I keep hearing those words: understand, respect, *ours*. But repetition doesn't give them meaning. I don't care how they want to remember her. "Do you really think…" I bite my tongue.

"Speak your mind, Corey," Mr. H says, his voice carefully pleasant.

"Do you really think she cared about a memorial? Don't you think she'd rather still *be here*?"

He flushes, and I expect him to yell at me. But after another heartbeat, his mouth thins and he nods. "Yes, I do think *my daughter* cared. She and I talked about this memorial, and I know she wanted you to be present. But you are not a necessity. We leave in thirty minutes."

I should feel badly for speaking to him so harshly, but I don't. I'm cycling through anger and grief and guilt and heartbreak. I'm homesick for a person, homesick for Kyra.

As I turn on my heels and head for the door, I overhear Mr. Henderson soothing his wife. "You know this was meant to be, don't you, Lynda? It's better this way. She's at peace."

Mrs. H's voice sounds tiny. "I know."

I close the door behind me, but I can't shut the conversation from my mind.

....

In the small cabin, I stare at myself in the mirror. The strapless black tunic I wear is the only piece of clothing I own that even remotely resembles a dress, and combined with a pair of dark jeans and a gray blazer, I hope it looks appropriate. Kyra wouldn't care, but Lost and I are mourning different people. The Kyra who died a week ago isn't the friend I left behind. Still, I lost them both.

I pick up my makeup bag and put on some foundation and mascara—just enough to not feel like a ghost myself. Then I dig around until I find the small jewelry purse I packed. My hands tremble, and the bracelet slips through my fingers the first two times, but I finally grab hold of it.

Kyra gave it to me before I left. It takes some messing with the clasp before it dangles around my wrist, but when it does, I feel calmer. *I could tell you stories about this*, she'd said when she gave it to me.

She never did.

Lost Creek insists on wearing pink, so I do the same. I put on a tourmaline petal charm Kyra made for me.

This new Lost doesn't seem real, but at least this piece of jewelry, this reminder of our friendship, isn't fake.

I look back into the mirror, and a sudden breeze plays with my hair, disheveling it. I don't know where it came from—not from an open window or the heating vent.

Kyra?

A chill runs down my spine as my heart aches. I grab my coat. It's time to leave for the memorial.

OF THE DEAD,
NOTHING BUT GOOD

THERE IS ICE BETWEEN MR. H AND ME WHEN WE LEAVE for Lost School. Maybe I should apologize. Except, I don't feel sorry. I stand by what I said. Kyra deserved more than this. She deserved more than these people claiming her, instead of accepting her. Now they mourn her without ever really having cared for her. And even if they had—or thought they had—seven months cannot undo years of scars.

The memorial service is held inside the gym of the school, and it's the first time I've been back inside this building that used to feel gigantic to me. It isn't. The space is hardly larger than the library at St. James, but it's big enough for everyone in Lost Creek.

From the moment we arrive, the Hendersons are the center of attention, and I'm surrounded by everyone I once knew. The people who, for sixteen years, had been more like family to me than my distant relatives who lived outside the borders of Lost. Mrs. Morden stands near the front of the room talking to Piper. Sheriff Flynn is present with his wife and Sam. In the corner, Jan, who runs the grocery store, is hovering around Mrs. Robinson, carefully keeping an eye on the old lady. Close by is Dr. Stevens, who cured more ills than cabin fever.

Even Aaron has shuffled into the building.

When I'd imagined what coming home would be like, it was this—familiar faces and, despite everything, smiles. It would be like that now, except that when I pass, people retreat. And I miss the two people who are obviously not here. Rowanne, who always came back for Kyra and always had a kind word for me.

And Kyra.

Then Mr. Sarin and Roshan walk in, filling the two empty spaces.

Everyone speaks in hushed tones. Beneath the cacophony of voices lies a more dangerous note. Someone hums the same tuneless song I heard when I first arrived, and it settles itself in my bones.

Occasionally, I pick up fragments of conversation. "It's a shame the family left town. I thought they knew better.

Look at her now. She doesn't belong here anymore. She doesn't fit in."

"She left. She shouldn't have come back."

"She doesn't understand us. She doesn't understand who Kyra was."

"Kyra was extraordinary."

"She doesn't understand who we are."

"I liked the boy, Luke. He respected our traditions. He didn't try to stand out like his sister. And at least with Kyra... Well, that was a whole different story, wasn't it?"

They glare at me, and I stare right back. Their words hurt me, but I won't let them see the bruises.

All I want is to see Kyra's smile. I slowly work my way toward the front of the gym, where I know I'll find flowers, and hopefully pictures too. But when the masses part before me, I wish I'd stayed put.

Kyra *is* here. Not in the flesh, of course, but in her art. Paintings, sketches, photographs of paintings that hang in the homes around town all decorate the inset stage. A colorful rendition of Lost Creek, brighter and happier than I've ever seen it. An image of the spa covered in flowers. The mine up north in production, apparently taken as a good thing despite the waste around it. A blazing star shooting through the night sky. I can't help but stare at this last piece. It doesn't fit with the collection. A supernova would be more apt. Or a black hole.

But the centerpiece is the painting that has been standing in the Hendersons' living room. The painting where Kyra foresaw her own death.

She's at peace. It was her time. The voices around me echo in my ears.

White-hot rage courses through me. At peace? She was *seventeen*. She spent most of her life fighting to belong. And she couldn't find that peace. Not even in Lost, a town that prides itself on being a home to the forgotten. It wasn't her time to die. It was her time to *live*.

Someone should have stopped her after she painted herself under the ice. They should have prevented this.

Someone rests a hand on my shoulder and I startle.

"It makes her look like she's dancing between the stars, doesn't it?" Piper says.

"It's a mockery. It's terrifying."

"She was happy, you know. At the end."

"Why does everyone keep saying that?" I hiss. I keep my voice low. "Why would anyone who's happy kill herself?"

"Because she found her purpose and served it. Don't you remember how she always wanted to change the world? She made a difference. She made Lost a better place to live." Piper's eyes flick to the crowd. "Isn't that all any of us can ask for?"

"She needed help, not a purpose. She needed friends."

"And yet you left her."

I slap her before I even realize what I'm doing. Gasps from somewhere behind me tell me it hasn't gone unnoticed, but I keep my stare trained on Piper, who merely shakes her head. She seems disappointed.

"I was part of her life for sixteen years," I seethe.

"But we were here when it mattered most."

"Don't tell me about friendship," I snap at her. "I was her friend."

"You were," she acknowledges. "Once upon another time."

....

At the microphone, Sheriff Flynn clears his throat and starts the memorial by directing us all to our seats. Mr. and Mrs. Henderson sit in a place of pride in the front row, directly in front of Mr. Sarin and Roshan, who are apparently guests of honor in Lost. The Flynns sit next to them, and on the other side of a small aisle sits Mrs. Morden, her son, and her grandchildren, Piper and Tobias. Everyone else finds seats among the rows of chairs, which make the space look like a small church.

I stay in the back, where I lean against a paneled wall. I'm too overwhelmed to sit. I think about what I'd said to Piper and Roshan at Claja. I'd honestly thought that Lost had taken the idea of not speaking ill of the dead to a whole new level. Now I know that it's more than politeness; it's a belief.

Sheriff Flynn talks us through the proceedings. There will be speakers, with the Hendersons last in line. After the formal part of the memorial, we'll have time to come together and remember Kyra's life. Mrs. Henderson baked a cake specially.

Mrs. Morden steps up onto a small stage and takes to the microphone, and everyone sits up straight.

"We never found God here in Lost," she begins, "but we did find Kyra."

NO NEED TO SAY GOODBYE

INT. LOST SCHOOL—GYM—DAY

A gymnasium, set with rows of chairs. Two hundred people or more are in attendance. The entire town, if some people are to be believed.

Mrs. Morden, owner of the town's post office, notable widow, and purveyor of fine gossip, stands at the microphone. She touches the magenta flower she's wearing, almost reverently.

Mrs. Morden

"Tell me a story." That's how our Kyra always started her observations. "Tell me a story about Lost, about the people you knew, about the endless snow around us. Tell me a story, and I will paint it for you." She gave us a past we'd forgotten and futures we couldn't yet see. She saw both at the same time.

"Tell me a story," she said, and we told her—

Crowd

We will obey.

The crowd collectively pauses to let their words reverberate through the gym as they touch the magenta flowers they all wear.

Mrs. Morden

For the longest time, we didn't understand Kyra. We all know how hard it could be to connect and to truly hear what she was saying. But once we came to understand her art, we came to

know her and to hear her messages. We
came to understand her love for this
home we've built.

Corey bites her tongue.

Mrs. Morden

Sometimes I wonder, and I know
I'm not alone in this, what would have
happened if we'd heard her sooner. Her
art gave her purpose, but she was with
us for such a short time, a bright star
that burned out.

What if we'd recognized what she'd
been trying to say from the beginning?
What if we'd acknowledged her?

But Kyra taught us that we cannot
change the past. We must look toward
the future. Life is what it is—

Crowd

And so be it.

Mrs. Morden

At least we can draw comfort from
knowing that we provided for her, for a

little while. We provided for her art and gave her all that she needed to create. She came home to us, built her home with us. She brightened our gray world. She made this community tighter, better.

We have no need to say goodbye. Kyra will never be far from us. She'll live on in her creations, and the town she left behind will be filled with her heart. We will continue her legacy. It is what it is—

Crowd

And so be it.

Mrs. Morden

"Tell me a story," Kyra said, and we told her—

Crowd

We will obey.

SCORN AND CELEBRATION

HALFWAY THROUGH THE REMEMBRANCES, THERE IS A short intermission. So far, with the exception of Mrs. Morden, none of the people who have spoken about Kyra were people I'd ever seen *with* Kyra. It hurts more and more to be unable to speak out, to be forced into this dance without knowing the steps.

When Piper appears at my side again, hers is the last face I want to see.

"Don't hit me again," she says, raising her hands. "I came to apologize."

I scowl. Does she really think making amends is that easy?

"No," she says, as if I'd asked the question out loud.

Maybe I did. "I don't think it's that easy. But I always considered you a friend. You were Kyra's friend. I behaved like an ass earlier, and I'm sorry."

Piper seems genuine, which makes it hard to stay angry at her. Still, "You did," I say. "And you may think that I abandoned her, but Kyra meant everything to me. Is that so hard to accept?"

She cocks her head. "No," she says. "But in return, is it so hard for you to accept in return that we truly cared about Kyra?"

"Yes. Yes, it is." The truth is, I'm starting to believe Lost Creek only *thinks* it cared about Kyra. I'm starting to think they *believed* they were doing right by her. I even think their intentions may have been good.

But intentions alone are never enough.

....

The memorial continues on, a performance, not a remembrance. Almost everyone in town speaks a few words to Kyra's memory. People who passed her by whenever she walked around town, who pretended she was invisible. People who demanded she be sent away. They all claim to have known and cared about her.

At first, I think Kyra would have been amused. It's as though they're talking about a world-famous artist, a traveling bard, someone larger than life.

She *did* want to change the world. She wanted to go on adventures, explore, collect stories. She wanted to love and lust. She wanted to volunteer and travel, if she could find the right combination of therapy and medication. She wanted to discover who she could be outside the borders of Lost.

After our kiss, after days of talking and not talking and talking some more, she holed up in the school's library, the only place in Lost with decent internet. She wanted to understand us, she said, and she came back with a whole list of orientations and identities. It was the first time I'd seen *asexuality* spelled out, and I found myself in the description.

Kyra claimed *pansexual*, and it fit her comfortably too. "I don't want my love to be limited," she told me. "I just want to love."

This was Kyra's story. She'd only just started it.

....

Collectively, the speakers talk for a *long* time. Given our scant hours of daylight in the winter, it's an unspoken rule to make the most of them. Today, daylight might as well have been ignored altogether. Night falls again.

"Do you understand now?" the people around me whisper, and the one thing I do understand is they want me to believe in the same world they see. But I can't, because that world no longer includes my best friend.

I can't believe it. And I won't. I start down the aisle.

I owe it to her to tell her story. I'll remember her on my own terms.

SERVICE, INTERRUPTED

INT. LOST SCHOOL—GYM—DUSK

Corey strides down the center aisle toward the front of the room. Onstage, she glares at the crowd.

Corey (*not loudly enough to be heard by all, but still loud enough*):
Let me tell you a story.

Let me tell you a story about a girl who lived in an abandoned spa, who cried for help and was refused it. Let me tell you a story about how she died.

Crowd

(Dead silence.)

Corey

Kyra was my best friend.

Aaron shifts in his seat, taking in the unrest around him. Following Corey's script, not the townspeople's, he rises and joins Corey onstage.

Aaron *(to Corey):*

Go. Now.

Aaron gently places a hand on Corey's shoulder and nudges her offstage. There's urgency in his touch and tension in his face. Corey stumbles, then walks off the stage and along the outer wall. When Aaron starts to speak, no one minds her anymore.

Aaron *(to the crowd, loudly)*:

Kyra was a good girl. She wasn't a messiah. She was lonely, and she was ill. She needed more than the food you brought her. She needed help. She needed hope. She needed people to see her and care about her instead of her art. That was hardly the most important aspect about her. She needed a chance. She did not have to die. This wasn't her story.

Aaron risks a glance at Corey before he turns to stare at the painting of Kyra's death.

Sheriff Flynn and Mr. Henderson get up and walk toward the stage in perfect synchrony. Mrs. Henderson wails into the silence.

Aaron *(turning to Mrs. Henderson)*:

This is not a celebration. She wasn't a star, and she didn't burn up. She was a good girl, and she deserved more.

Aaron walks offstage, dignified but determined, then out of the building.

Chaos erupts. Sheriff Flynn swears and Mrs. Henderson collapses. Piper dashes forward to support her. Mr. Henderson stares at the door where Aaron left, his expression thoughtful and cold. The crowd whispers accusations, and there are more tears.

Corey holds her head low and edges toward the door, pulling her coat off a table in the back. Before anyone can stop her, she dashes out into the cold.

DARKNESS FALLS

"AARON!"

My voice echoes between the empty houses. Daylight disappeared while we were inside, and Aaron is nowhere to be seen. I scan the road for footprints, but the snow is trampled and dirty. From here, it's an easy trek through the woods to the spa. If I were him, I wouldn't go back to Lost. I'd go home.

I zip my parka and pick up a firm pace. Once darkness truly falls, it'll be too dangerous to go through the woods alone, but Aaron is the only one with the answers I need. He all but said the town killed Kyra.

"Aaron!" I call again when I reach the tree line, but

the only response is silence. That only freaks me out more. The woods aren't supposed to be silent, not even in winter. Silence is a sign of danger, of lurking predators. We're taught that from a very young age.

"Aaron!"

Nothing.

I continue along the path. I know it well—Kyra dragged me here so many times—and my footing is almost instinctive. Still, darkness falls fast around me, and with every step deeper into the woods, I feel like I leave safety farther behind. This is one of the few places in Lost where the sky grows midnight-dark as soon as the sun sets. And that's when the wolves come out.

I know I should go back. I have no weapons, no flashlight, not even my phone to use for light.

I keep walking. Aaron looked distraught. Maybe he'll tell me what I need to hear so I can go home.

The trees close in around me. The silence lengthens, until the wind picks up. It's an eerie sound, the wind through the trees, and just as oppressing as the silence. Yet there's no rustling of leaves or pine needles. Instead, it sounds like the same tune, over and over again. Always.

Endless day, endless night.
Come to set your heart alight.
Endless night, endless day.
Come to steal your soul away.

Endless night, endless day.

Come to set your heart alight.

Come to steal your soul away.

The last light shifts and a shadow crosses mine. Off the path, something moves. I stifle a scream and leap out of the way. *A hand? An arm?* My heart beats double time.

A branch, nothing more.

Then I see the eyes.

Owl eyes first. Then cat eyes.

Yellow eyes.

Human eyes.

They're all pinpricks of light in the darkness.

Only the owl is blinking, slowly. Everything else— everyone else—simply stares.

The wind hums Kyra's tune and eyes are everywhere I turn. Watching me. Watching me, and waiting.

But for what, I don't know.

Then, as if they've heard some signal I can't hear or see, they drift closer, slowly but steadily. The lights—the eyes—bar my path to the spa. They surround me.

"Aaron?" My voice falters and breaks.

Whatever happened out on the ice, Kyra wouldn't want me to die in these woods. So, as the eyes begin to tighten their circle, I back away. And I run.

A BACKPACK FULL OF HOME

WHEN I RETURN TO THE HENDERSONS', THE HOUSE IS
still dark and empty. I don't even care. I don't want to
see them. I don't want to see anyone. I want to leave.

I never fully unpacked, so repacking my bag is easy.
It's too late to find a way to Fairbanks now, but first
thing tomorrow morning, when the reception clears,
I'll call the airline to reschedule my flight. I've been to
the memorial service. What more can I really hope to
achieve?

Don't go, she wrote on the walls of her room.

I'm sorry, Kyra. Maybe everyone who has called
me an outsider was right; I long for the yellow light of

the city. I long for my dorm room. I long for the border between worldly and otherworldly to be clearly defined.

I'll leave a piece of myself here. And no matter where I go, even if Lost is no longer my home, I will still be an Alaskan. This landscape has shaped who I am, even if this community is no longer my own.

I put Kyra's notes and drawings in my backpack, and with them, Kyra's scarf. I couldn't leave them at the spa. They're too personal. I'm taking them, taking Kyra with me. It's the least I can do.

Hers is a story that deserves to be told. Hers is a story that deserves to be heard. It's the story of a girl who believed in heroes and wanted to be one herself. Who saw stories in the world around her, and who regaled an entire Alaskan town with them. And hers is a story of how they started to believe her.

THE SMELL OF SMOKE

MY EYES BURN. ARMS HEAVY FROM SLEEP, I REACH UP and rub at my eyes. Blink.

My throat burns. I try to swallow and cough instead. I can't stop coughing.

I gulp in air, but it's acrid. Smoke. My brain freezes. *Smoke.*

I'm surrounded by a darkness deeper than any night I've experienced. I reach for my phone but come back empty. A trail of flames starts eating its way across the ceiling, through the doorway that's now open to Kyra's room.

I can't breathe.

The building is on fire. And I'm inside it.

THE TASTE OF ASHES

I HAVE TO GET OUT.

I stand and buckle under the weight of the hot air. My face feels like it's blistering. I have to get out. I have to keep my wits about me and *get out*. If not through the door, then the window.

I hold my breath against the smoke and try to pull up the sill. It's jammed. Another coughing fit wrecks me. I grab the desk chair and hurl it at the window. It shatters, but shards of glass stick out from the frame.

My throat closes and my eyes have gone completely dry.

I grab my backpack and charge at the window, pushing away as much glass as I can. The heat makes it easy to focus on my priorities. I'd rather cut myself to shreds than get burned alive. *Like a witch*, Kyra once said.

The sudden influx of cold air burns my hands, but the flames feel like they're at my back and crawling up my legs, so I dive forward using my backpack as a shield.

I let myself fall.

In the yard, the snow and the cold are at once overwhelming and welcoming. I sliced my palm and tore open my shin, but I'm *out*. I gasp for air. It hurts to breathe. My throat is raw from smoke and screaming. It hurts to *be*.

Kyra's piece of home burns before my eyes. These walls held memories and happiness. We made plans here, and dreamed. We slogged through mountains of homework. We were together. *We were together.* And now, it's going up in flames. I lost her, and now I'm losing this too.

I push myself away from the building and collapse against my backpack, strangely relieved to have my clothes with me. At school, they taught us how to handle fire drills—to leave coats and bags and other belongings behind. But I cling to the few familiar things I have left.

I brace myself for another coughing fit. I would shout for help again, but everything hurts. Besides, we have no proper fire department in town. What could anyone do? The blaze is beyond the reach of a fire extinguisher or makeshift brigade. But the town always sticks together in moments like these. We cling to solidarity, even when there is no hope.

They'll be here any moment now, I tell myself.

I close my eyes as the world around me spins. I breathe in the night air and wait for the cold to numb the pain.

The Hendersons' house remains dark and still. I try to shout, but I can't. I try to get up to run, but I can't. I want to cry, but I can't.

The only movement I see is the flames licking at the roof. Nothing else.

Only when I finally struggle to my feet do I find a crowd gathered in the side yard. Lost is here. Watching. Waiting. Silent.

At the forefront stands Mr. H. He stares at me, but he doesn't acknowledge me. He doesn't move to help me. He doesn't move at all.

In his hands, he holds Kyra's scarf. The scarf that had been tucked inside my backpack.

DAY FOUR

WHERE DO WE GO FROM HERE?

I MIGHT AS WELL BE A GHOST, BECAUSE NO ONE PAYS attention to me. They don't aid me, they don't try to stop me when I stumble out of the yard. It's like I don't exist anymore. I can't stay in this town.

I walk in a daze. The woods aren't safe at night, even with a path to follow, but Lost isn't safe anymore either. I need a sanctuary. *It is what it is.*

I cough again and it feels as though I'm breathing liquid fire.

I don't know how much time passes. I don't even know if time passes at all or if the world moves without me, but eventually I stagger into the spa. Moonlight filters in through the tall windows, and the entrance hall is clad in shadows. I still don't have a flashlight to light the way. Even if I still had my phone, it'd be melted plastic and glass. I always thought I knew this place so well I could find my way around blindfolded, but now that I'm inside, navigating in the dark is difficult.

I feel my way to the staircase and stumble upstairs. I can't stop shivering.

Reaching the landing, I start toward Kyra's room, but I can't stay there. Not tonight.

My footsteps echo. The hotel breathes around me, but I hold my breath. A sigh tickles the back of my neck.

I shudder. "Who's there?"

The floorboards creak. But I can't see anyone. I trail my hand along the wall until I reach a doorpost. The first door doesn't open. The second door doesn't either. I don't want to know what lies behind them. The third door opens. I nearly sob in relief when I find a window and moonlight streaming in. It's not much light, but it's enough. I can see an ancient bed in the far corner.

I don't even care about not having blankets. I doubt I'll be able to sleep, and I'll wrap myself in my parka to stay warm.

I lie down on the bed and cradle my backpack. I stare into the darkness of the hall. I don't dare close the door, because I don't want to lock myself in, but the emptiness is unnerving. I'm sure that as soon as I take my eyes from the doorway, someone will appear in the darkness.

Is this how Kyra felt when she stayed here?

I remember her words, written on the walls of her room. *They're watching. The shadows, Corey. They're always watching.*

I thought she'd meant the shadows and haunts of this building. I never stopped to think "they" may have been real. But if so, who were they? Her parents? Her petitioners? All of Lost?

Lost stood by and would have let me burn. They would've been happy to watch her die too.

NOTE FROM KYRA TO COREY
UNSENT

It started so innocuously: a painting of your brother and a wounded bird. At least, I think that's where it started. I can't remember who called it magical first.

Do you still have it?

I know you loved it, but I wish you had let me destroy it.

This isn't my story.

harm you. They won't hurt you. She was the storyteller of the two of us, and I am only weaving nightmares.

She would tease me, make me laugh to stop the fear from settling in. She would stay with me while I'm too afraid to move. She would make me feel strong enough to leave this place.

I miss her. And I want to go home.

Outside, the dark blues of twilight grow lighter.

I change into cleaner clothes—though everything of mine smells of smoke—and settle into one of the armchairs in the entryway. I have granola bars in my backpack. I have Kyra's portable heater. I have air in my lungs.

I'm not alone. Kyra's paintings and sketches surround me, and I can't stop leafing through them. Most are scenes I've never seen, of the private lives of the people of Lost. Some depict moments I've lived. Kyra and I skinny-dipping in the lake. Two little girls fishing, sitting side by side, arms around each other's shoulders. And eventually, Kyra alone, in this very same chair, surrounded by paintings.

I hug the papers close.

The first colonial settlers in Lost found that winter is not malleable, and frost settles too, Kyra once told me. *And no matter how hard they tried, they could not escape being lost... And they could not escape Lost.*

I always thought those were two separate things, but now I understand they're really not.

216

POLAR TWILIGHT

THE NIGHT PASSES SLOWLY. BY EARLY MORNING, I'M s
tired I doze off, my arms still wrapped around n
backpack. I dream of fire and heat, but when I wake, t
room is freezing cold. The shadows have yet to dissip
and whenever I turn from the door, I feel the dark
creeping closer. It's like the walls have eyes. *Th
always watching*, Kyra wrote.

I used to love that Lost is surrounded by nothi
nature for miles. It made us learn to be self-suf
self-reliant. Or so I thought.

All I want now is a friend.

I want Kyra to be here, to tell me, *The sha(*

NIGHT SWIMMING

THREE YEARS BEFORE

WE SLEPT, CURLED TOGETHER ON HER BED. OR RATHER, she lay awake while I slept. Well past midnight, the mattress shook as she climbed over me, then left the room. I didn't think anything of it and was fading back to sleep when I heard the door open and shut. *Where is Kyra going?*

I wrapped myself in a coat, slipped on shoes, and followed her outside.

The river had broken up a few weeks before, but snow still covered the ground, so I could easily trace her footprints. That was my first sign that something was wrong—it didn't look like she was wearing shoes.

I picked up my pace and ran after her, but she had a head start. And by the time I reached the shores of the lake, she'd already waded in.

I screamed, "Kyra!" And again, "Help!"

Up to her waist in the water, Kyra didn't turn or acknowledge my presence.

I discarded my coat and carefully walked in her direction. The edge of the lake was shallow and still frozen. The ice crackled under my weight, and the water that lapped at my feet was freezing.

I screamed for help again, but Kyra had already pushed off into the deep end. She let herself float, surrounded by chunks of ice. "I want to go swimming, Cor," she called.

"Come back! You'll die!"

I waded in farther. Tendrils of cold curved around my calves, and I was shivering. *I won't be able to get to her in time*, I panicked. *I won't be able to get to her in time.*

I needed help. And I didn't want to leave her.

But I made my way back to shore, picked up my coat from the snow, and ran to the nearest house to wake Lost.

By the time Mr. Henderson, Sheriff Flynn, and Mom got Kyra out of the water, she was chilled to the bone and hovering on the brink of unconsciousness. Severe hypothermia. Dr. Stevens had her flown to the hospital in

Fairbanks. Kyra had nearly died because she'd wanted to go swimming and I hadn't been able to stop her.

That was the first time someone mentioned mania.

That summer, Kyra went for a walk in the woods and went missing for three days straight. The entire town mobilized to comb the woods to find her, and by the time we did, she was covered in dirt and had a deep gash along her arm.

Then there was the time she fell off the spa's roof while trying to fly and broke her ankle and her collarbone.

And there was nothing I could do.

Kyra's hero days weren't always heroic. Her highs boosted her, but they could hurt her as much as her lows did. She lost just as much of herself to them, and it took me far too long to see that.

"Maybe that's why I long for stories," she confided in me, after she had to stop her first regimen of medication. The side effects had been plentiful, but without any of the benefits. She'd struggled with memory loss and constant nausea. "Stories remind me of heroes and possibilities. Stories remind me that I'm not the only one to deal with this. Stories make me feel less alone."

TESTIMONY

WHEN I WAKE AGAIN, ALL I SEE IS A GLOWING RED through my eyelids. They slowly flutter open, and I startle, goose bumps flushing my arms. A flashlight. My heart races, but I'm too terrified to scream.

Then the light lowers. Sheriff Flynn hovers a few feet away, flashlight in one hand, a paper bag and thermos in the other. I can't tell if the fleeting look that crosses his features is one of relief or disappointment that I'm okay.

My gut tells me to run, but where would I go? He stands between me and the doorway, and I can see the glint of his gun, holstered at his hip, as he sets the flashlight on the table beside him.

"Corey," he says gently.

This is the voice of the Sheriff Flynn who checked on Luke and me when Mom was away for work. Who was Mom's shoulder to lean on after Dad left five years ago. Still, Lost has threatened me, and he is part of that.

"Corey," he says again.

I wrap my sweater tighter around me. "What do you want?"

"I want to talk to you about what happened last night. May I?" He gestures to the chair next to mine.

I nod because I can't really refuse. Sheriff Flynn looks like he hasn't slept much either. Crime doesn't usually keep him up at night, not in this town. We have nothing more to worry about than the occasional drunkard, the occasional bear, and Kyra's manias. Now we don't even have that.

"Why are you here?" I try to keep my voice even, but it cracks around the edges.

Sheriff Flynn pulls an end table between us and puts the bag on it, pulling out buttered rolls wrapped in paper napkins. The smell of freshly baked bread hangs in the damp air.

My stomach growls.

"We've gotten used to bringing over food." Sheriff Flynn smiles, and with those few words, my appetite disappears. But my hands are shaking. I have to eat *something*.

I bite my lip. "What happened last night, Sheriff?"

"That's what I came here to ask you. How are you, Corey?"

I grab a roll and pick at it, breaking off small chunks of crust to nibble. "Scared."

Sheriff Flynn produces a notebook and scribbles something down. So much for empathy—he has a job to do. "Are you in pain?"

"I'm not burned, but I inhaled a lot of smoke," I say. As if my lungs want to prove it, I start coughing again. The memory of not being able to breathe is almost as potent as actual breathlessness. "Should I see a doctor?"

"You should have been examined last night, but you disappeared before Dr. Stevens arrived."

Sheriff Flynn sounds apologetic, but what he's saying is blatantly absurd. Dr. Stevens could've come for me at any point in the past several hours; it wouldn't have been hard to track me. But I nod because it still hurts to breathe and I'm too tired to argue.

"She would like you to come in. I'll walk you there after our talk."

"What happened to Kyra's cabin, Sheriff?"

"The fire was contained, so it didn't spread to the main house or any of the surrounding structures. The guest room and Kyra's room were completely destroyed, unfortunately." His words are cold. Emotionless.

"I was inside. I could've *died*." Saying it out loud makes my hands tremble so hard I have to ball my fingers into fists so the sheriff won't notice. My sliced palm burns.

Sheriff Flynn doesn't even look up from his notes.

"Do you know what caused the fire?" I ask. This town has now burned down the two places I considered home. *Was that foretold too?* I want to ask.

He shakes his head. "I'm no forensic expert when it comes to fires, so I can't give you a definitive answer, but we've seen this before, Corey. Space heaters that overheat. Electrical malfunctions. It was likely an accident, nothing more."

"Like Kyra," I mutter. The town may not want to murder me, but they're certainly not above an intentional mishap.

At this, Sheriff Flynn looks up from his notebook. "Excuse me?"

I wince, and he continues. "It's lucky you discovered the fire as soon as you did." His voice sounds flat. Maybe he thinks it would've been luckier still if people in town had found a way to stop me from asking my nosy questions.

"Can I get out of here?" I keep my voice flat too, but inside I'm trembling. "I want to go home to my family."

"Joe called the airline, but the next plane that will route through Lost is the one you've already booked your flight on. You can wait in town or here, if you'd prefer."

"I'll stay here." I don't have to think about that.

Sheriff Flynn nods, clearly not surprised. "We'll make sure you have food, of course. Do you have everything else you need? Blankets, heater?"

"I'm fine." I may not be comfortable using Kyra's things, but I'm even less comfortable accepting help from Lost. At least Kyra never wished me harm.

I pick up another roll, and although I don't have a taste for it, eating keeps my hands busy. "Has anyone called my mom to tell her what happened?"

The mood in the room shifts. "Did you not call her? As far as I know, no one else has been in contact with her. She hasn't called me."

He cocks his head with a glint in his eyes, and for a second, he reminds me of a hawk, or a vulture. And *I'm* the prey. There would be no witnesses if I died or disappeared. The town would get what it wanted.

I put the roll down on a napkin and brush the crumbs from my hands. "No, sorry. She expects to hear from me. I promised to call each day."

I don't know if I'm convincing, but I don't think he'll call my bluff. I don't know what will happen if I stay here until my flight. But maybe that will be the safety I need until then. I still don't know Kyra's side of the story—and part of me is still waiting for the clues that will help her tell it.

I cannot abandon my friend again.

I set my jaw. "Tell me, Sheriff. Am I in danger here?"

"Why would you think that? Of course not. As I said, the fire was an accident. Regrettable, but nothing more. We'll provide for you until you leave."

I can't sit through any more of these lies. I stand and flip through some of Kyra's sketches that cover the big table, then pick up a sketch of the sheriff's son smiling and flash it at him. "How is Sam?" I narrow my eyes and find a painting of the mines. "How is business in Lost?"

The temperature drops noticeably, and it wasn't warm to begin with. I shiver, but I stare down the sheriff. I almost *died*.

Sheriff Flynn closes his notebook. "Why are you are unwilling to let this go, Corey?"

He stands and pulls on his coat, sliding his notebook and pen inside his breast pocket, but he leaves the bag of food and the thermos.

"Walk with me. I'll show you to Dr. Stevens," he says, his words measured. "And after that, stick to the spa. You're not one of us anymore."

I can't tell if he's angry or defeated, but right then and there, I don't care.

He's right. I'm not one of them anymore, and that's almost a relief.

A CURE FOR ALL ILLS

Sheriff Flynn leads me through town in silence. I'm sure everyone knows about the fire, but no one cares enough to ask if I'm all right. People stare at me. They whisper. Mr. Lucas touches the magenta flower he's still wearing, and his lips move silently, as if in prayer, when he sees me.

Is this what it was like for Kyra all those years? They feared her because she was different. They saw her as less because she was ill. Suddenly appreciating her art does not clear the stain of their silence. Especially if they never acknowledged her for who she was as a person.

We were here when it mattered most, Piper said at the memorial.

But she's wrong. They were there for Kyra when it was profitable for them and they had something to gain. If they'd been there for her when it mattered, they'd have been with her long before she ventured out onto the ice. They would have been there when she struggled to adjust to new medication. When she cried herself to exhaustion because she hadn't slept in days. When she was too scared to talk about the future because she was convinced she'd never escape the darkness—never escape Lost.

If the people of Lost had been with Kyra when it mattered most, they would've been there for her on those days between mania and depression, when she could step away from her art and her fear. They would've talked to her, they would've cared for her, not as the beneficent, bipolar daughter of the Hendersons, but as Kyra, one of their own.

That's when it mattered most.

They weren't here when it mattered most.

But I can't help but think that neither was I. If I had been with Kyra when it mattered, I would've called, answered her letters. I would've been a safe haven when Lost turned her into a prophet, and I would've found a way to get her out. I would not be trying to understand how she died.

If any of us had been here when it mattered most, she would still be alive.

....

Sheriff Flynn leaves me on my own at Dr. Stevens's house, but despite her insistence that I come see her, she is out, according to her assistant, Meghan. Meghan can only give me vague estimates and water and aspirin for the headache that's taken up residence behind my eyes. From oxygen deprivation, maybe? Or anger?

"I'm sorry I can't do more for you," she says, while she sorts through medical charts, filing paperwork. She moves them from one stack to another, slowly, methodically. "You're welcome to wait." With a large manila envelope, she gestures at the double bench that functions as a waiting room.

"You don't know how much longer Dr. Stevens will be?"

"No. It may be a while."

Her tone reminds me of the one I used with Sheriff Flynn when I mentioned calling my mother this morning, and I'm almost certain that she's lying. Maybe Dr. Stevens *is* only out for an errand. Maybe, despite what Meghan says, she's in the building, though it's hard to imagine Dr. Stevens sitting on the other side of the door, waiting for me to walk out. I've always known her as helpful and caring. But I can't be sure if I'm safe to leave. I don't want to risk my health.

"It's okay." I shake my head. "Thanks for the painkillers."

I place the empty glass on Meghan's desk. She casually drops a magenta flower into it.

I shiver. It makes no sense to bring me back to town, only to make me hang out in a waiting room—unless Sheriff Flynn, or any of the others, wanted me out of the spa.

Meghan smiles a crooked smile, and I think of the few times Mom brought me here. When I had bronchitis, Meghan brewed me tea with honey to help soothe my throat. When I was seven and sprained my ankle running with Kyra, she told me bad jokes to distract me from the pain.

But now she's silent as I wait. And wait.

Meghan is still stacking and restacking folders, what feels like an hour later. It's an endless process, and I don't see how she's changing anything. She's just keeping busy and humming quietly to herself.

Finally, I give up and walk toward the door.

"Maybe you should spend some time at the hot springs," she suggests without looking up. "They are said to cure all ills." Then she resumes her humming, though louder.

Behind Meghan hangs a sketch that shows her alongside her two sons, both of whom left Lost years ago.

I laugh, and it's painful in my lungs, but I can't stop. At least not until I'm outside and sobs overtake my laughter. Her humming echoes in my ears. It's the song I first heard at the airport. The song that now floats in the air all around me.

Come to steal your soul away.

Someone, out of sight, begins to hum. It's the same song Corey hears everywhere, and it has an ominous tone. It's loud, as if the sound comes from the stones and the trees around her, not just from the people of Lost.

Tobias barrels into Corey on the street. She stumbles. He doesn't turn or apologize. He keeps walking.

Along Main, Corey sees Mr. Henderson and Sheriff Flynn at the edge of town. They're deep in conversation. She can see their mouths move, but she can't hear them.

Piper

Corey?

Corey turns to find Piper staring at her from across the street. Mud from Mrs. Robinson's garden covers her clothes and her hair. She glances up and down the street, then walks over at a brisk pace.

FEAR ABOUT TOWN

EXT. LOST CREEK—MAIN STREET—END OF DAY

Corey walks through Lost at a brisk pace, while everyone stares silently at her. The whole town falls still.

Corey *(frustrated with the lack of help, in pain, to no one in particular)*:

Is this how you treat each other? Kyra was no oracle. She was sick, and she needed help. Does no one understand that?

Piper *(reaching out to touch*
Corey's arm):

I saw you stumble. Are you okay?

Corey

No.

She turns away from Piper, but Piper pulls
her back. She is gentle, but insistent.

Piper

We're all afraid in our own way.

In the distance, Roshan, who had started
to make his way toward Corey, observes
the conversation with a frown. With
Piper around, he pushes his hands deep
into his pockets and stalks away.

It begins to snow.

EMPTY ROOMS, LOST WORDS

I WOULD RUN BACK TO THE HOT SPRINGS IF I COULD breathe properly. Instead, I walk as fast as I can.

The falling snow is creating a thick, new carpet. When I enter the spa, I stomp my boots before closing the door behind me. I stare. The grand entrance is empty. The hall that resembled a shrine when I left a few hours ago is now nothing more than a hall. There are no paintings, no sketches, no candles, no salmonberry blossoms. The chairs and table still stand around the hearth, but that's all that remains.

A thin layer of dust coats the hard surfaces, which makes it look like no one has been here for months.

What happened while I was gone? Am I hallucinating this? Is it a side effect of smoke inhalation?

I draw lines on the table, and my fingers come back dusty. It's as if Kyra had never been here.

Far behind me, faint giggles echo through the building.

If someone was here, are they still here now?

If I'm going to survive two more nights in this place, I need to know I'm the only one in the spa. Even if that means checking every single room. So I start at the large reception area at the side of the entrance. This way no one can sneak up on me from rooms I haven't cleared, and I can bolt if there is danger. No one will be between me and the exit. Though where I would go if I had to escape, I don't know.

In the dining room, fresh salmonberry flowers are spread out over every windowsill. Dust reveals half-disappeared footprints on the floor. I seem to be alone, but what am I supposed to make of this?

I work my way through the old building. Most of the rooms remain untouched, exactly as I remember them from all my visits with Kyra.

But some of the rooms still bear witness to Kyra's presence. The walls in the room where Kyra slept are still covered with her writing. And in this brighter light, I can see that other rooms in this wing harbor Kyra's writing too. In the room next door:

They're watching. They're watching. They're
always watching.

And in the corner:

Even the walls have eyes.

In the next room, it's one word. Over and over again.

Goodbye. Goodbye. Goodbye. Goodbye.

Down the hall, the writing becomes mostly endless loops,
like when we practiced cursive writing in school. Based on
the different colors of ink, and the way some of the lines
fade, she must have made her way through half a dozen
pens, and it's a lonely sight. Then, around the doorway:

Come get me, please. Or I'll come to you.

In the last room, the walls are bare, except for two
scrawled words, large and frantic:

Mom. Please.

I have to stop. The weight of Kyra's unanswered pleas
is crushing me. I sit down in the middle of the otherwise

empty space. The floorboards creak. I put my head in my hands.

And I break.

I hurt more fiercely than I ever have before. And I cry. I cry for the girl I used to know, who turned this rotten building into her superhero headquarters and tried to help a world that didn't want to help her.

I cry for the girl I used to know, who kept my heart in the palm of her hands.

I cry for the girl I used to know, who hated to paint and spent the last months of her life in a space filled with her paintings.

But most of all, I cry for the girl who used to be my world, who deserved to have the galaxy at her feet.

I would give up every single star in the night sky to have another day with her.

DEAR DIARY

She won't come back. She won't come back. She'll never come back.

I replay the same scenarios in my mind: Kyra in her room, writing on the walls. Kyra in the hall, accepting food and flowers from her petitioners. Painting to cope.

Kyra, alone.

Kyra, writing me letters. I still have unanswered letters at St. James and back at Mom's house. I still have so many things I should have written her, but I never did. I never even said goodbye.

The flood of tears leaves me empty and spent. My

shoulders and neck ache from crying. My eyes burn. I don't know how to go on from here.

Restless energy overtakes me. I can't sit still.

I scramble to my feet and wander along the other rooms on this floor, but they're all empty, the only color on the walls that of half-torn wallpaper. I explore the wing where my own room is and find nothing.

In the other wing, the rooms are dustiest. No words. No signs of life. I came here yesterday hoping to miraculously find Kyra. Now, I open every door with the expectation that it will be empty. *She'll never come back.*

Until I find myself on the north side of the building. *We're safe here*, Kyra told me, the very first time we dared to venture to the spa on our own.

I push open the door and it squeaks in its hinges.

Gray light filters into the room through the window and French doors, which lead out to a balcony. Shadows dance on the walls. And the floor is covered with footprints.

I kneel down and trace one. *Kyra.*

How has it only been a week since she died? It feels like I lost her long before then. Maybe I did.

The footprints go back and forth between the door to the hallway and the doors to the balcony. I pull the sleeves of my knit sweater over my hands and push out to the balcony.

A layer of snow blankets it. The metal railing that surrounds it is cold through my sleeves, and the wind bites. The snow keeps falling, fresh and thick, covering everything around me.

From here, Kyra and I had the best view of the hot springs and the surrounding woods. In daylight, you can see the snowcapped peaks in the distance. Now, the mountains are shapeless shadows in the slate gray sky. I turn west, to try to make out Lost Creek, but all I see is the end of a broken road that leads from the spa to the town.

Did Kyra sit up here and watch the townspeople approach the spa? Did she dread it, when she saw them? Did she try to escape?

I rub at my eyes and stumble back into the room, pulling hard on the doors to close them. As I start to leave, I remember the loose floorboard where we used to keep our stash of chocolate. I wrench it away and feel around underneath it. At first, there's nothing but splinters. When I push a little deeper, I feel something soft and smooth. I angle my hand to get a better hold and pull out a small leather-bound notebook. The blue cover and the edges of the pages are stained, and when I flick through it, most have been torn from the spine. But all the pages that are left are filled from margin to margin.

UNSENT

Dear Corey,

I moved to the spa. I claimed one of the upstairs bedrooms. It's dank and more than a little dusty, but I brought my notebooks and pens, and Mom will bring me my books.

The spa feels like a haven—or a headquarters. Lost has changed so much these last couple of months, you probably wouldn't recognize it if you were here. I'm not sure if I recognize it. Or if I recognize myself.

The townspeople though, they see me now. Not just my parents and Aaron and Mrs. Robinson, but all of them. They don't scorn me with their sideways glances. They _see_ me. They see _me_.

I can be useful to them. I can paint the scenes they want to see. I can create a way to belong here.

It's a sun—bright hero day, and the night feels far away and distant. I feel alive.

I wish you could see me like this.

I'm spiraling, Cor. Fall is setting in and the nights are getting longer, but my days are still endless. Endless days. No nights. And I miss the darkness, but I can't sit still. I can't stop. I have to keep going.

I thought Lost saw me, but they only see my art. They all want to see paintings, and most of the time I don't even remember painting them. I wish you were here. I wish I had a way to contact you beyond the letters Aaron sends out for me, but the spa doesn't have a phone or reception, and I can't go home. They wouldn't let me.

I just want someone to talk to.

I wish you would come sooner, because I'm so tired. I can't sleep. I'm burning. I wish you would come sooner. I don't know if I can wait.

I will wait.

I wish I could tell you how much I miss you.

Dear Corey,

They took away my stories and my books, and left me only with paints. This notebook is my secret, so now you are my diary.

Writing to you has become the start of my day and the end of it. I've written you so many letters. I'm not sure what Dad reads, so I'll only send you the safe ones, where my real messages are written between the lines. The rest—these letters, I won't risk sending. But maybe it doesn't matter. I've gotten used to your silences.

Perhaps you'll read this one day. I hope you

will. And perhaps it will be easier for me to write without expecting an answer. I still hope and pray that I can tell you this story in person one day, but in case I can't.

Here goes.

Remember when we danced on the ice before you left? Remember how I told you stories about Lost Creek? I've never been a good storyteller, I know that. I'd much rather study stories than tell them. But I always thought we'd make our own legends.

Let me tell you a story.

There once was a lonely girl who lived in an abandoned spa, among candles and flowers and offerings. She didn't belong in the community around her, but when she carved out her own space, the people came to her. For stories and secrets and art.

There once was a boy who never smiled. Everyone who knew him knew that he was searching, but he didn't know what he was looking for, so he couldn't find it—or happiness.

The boy who never smiled visited the lonely girl who lived in the abandoned spa. Unlike the others, he came just to be. And the girl was relieved. And she told him that sometimes the things we hope to find are things that must come to us instead. And not long after, a stranger came to town who brought

HISTORY

A YEAR AND A HALF BEFORE

"Do you believe in God?" I asked Kyra. We sat on the dock of White Wolf Lake, our feet dangling in the water, the summer sun hot on our faces.

"Yes. Sometimes. Maybe?" She shrugged. "There's more that exists outside the borders of Lost, so why shouldn't that hold true for the borders of this world and this life? Besides, what is religion if not a collection of myths and legends? Stories to help explain the unknown?"

I tilted my head a little. "Then what do you believe in?"

The corner of her mouth pulled up in a wry half smile.

the boy what he needed. And for the first

the boy smiled.

There once was a lonely girl who lived i

abandoned spa. She spent her days waiting. Wa

for the townspeople to visit her, and waiting

them to leave again. Because while she'd hoped t

would bring her the friendship she longed for, t

brought her flowers and candles, and then left w

her hope.

Let me tell you a story.

There once was a lonely girl who lived in a

abandoned spa. The people used her, drained her o

all she had to give, until she had nothing left.

I have nothing left.

I'm scared, Cor.

Come back to me.

"I don't know, exactly. I like the idea of a benevolent god. God is love? I can believe that. But I want my life to have meaning because I give it meaning, not because someone else says that it does. I want my life to mean something because I create. Because I love. Because I make the world a better place."

"I believe in the universe." I hesitated. "I believe in you."

She turned to me, but her eyes strayed to a point far behind me. "Do you?" she asked quietly. "Do you believe in me? Or do you believe in my manic episodes?"

"Kyra…"

"I know we have our hero days, but it's not my bipolar disorder that makes me want to change the world. It's me. Do you believe that I can?"

"Life just seems a lot easier when you're…"

"When I'm manic and bursting with energy? Have you ever not slept for days on end? All I hear are a million stories, but I can't sit still long enough to write them down. All I see are images that demand to be committed to paper because otherwise they'll claw their way out through my skin." She spoke loud and fast, her words flowing from emotion, not mania. "Trust me, those episodes aren't easier. I'm more productive, but it isn't because I'm happier. It's because I'll burn up if I'm not busy. And I'm never busy with the work I really want to produce."

I flinched. I'd never noticed that Kyra didn't paint

when she was depressed or between episodes. And I hadn't considered whether or not she liked to paint. I'd never thought to ask. And I didn't want to admit that.

Kyra sighed, and when she spoke again, her voice was soft and low. "It isn't easier when life goes flat, either. When my moods turn dark and it feels like the sun won't rise again."

"I…" Kyra's nights scared me. The idea of losing her scared me. Not knowing how to fix that darkness scared me.

"I have to be able to talk about my illness—my episodes—without you jumping to conclusions."

"I don't jump to conclusions." I paused and shook my head. "I do. I'm sorry."

"I'm not a puzzle to solve, you know."

Her words hit me hard. "I know. I don't want to solve you, I want to help you. I don't want to see you hurt."

"You're my friend. All I need you to do is be here with me. I don't want you to flinch away from me."

I turned to her and stared directly into her hazel eyes. "I really am sorry."

She nods. "I know."

ALLIES

I MAKE IT THROUGH HALF THE LETTERS BEFORE I RUN TO the bathroom and throw up the meager breakfast I'd eaten. My head is spinning. I need fresh air. I need to get out.

I head toward Aaron's cabin. The closer I get to it, the stronger it smells of sulfur from the hot springs, although I imagine he's used to it.

Aaron's door stands ajar. Snow has blown in, dusting the floor. I frown. *Weird.* Knocking, I let myself in. "Aaron?"

The cabin is a small, square building, with tiny, square rooms. A living room. A kitchen. A bedroom. A bathroom. All for the keeper of the spa. And it's quiet. Too quiet.

A breeze as light as a sigh caresses the back of my neck.

"Aaron?" I try again. My voice trips and breaks.

A small, half-built model airplane sits on the kitchen table. A tiny jar of paint is open, and a brush rests on top of it. I pick it up. The hairs have gone hard and the paint in the jar has dried out.

I saw Aaron yesterday, but it seems like he hasn't been here for some time.

I walk to the coffee table and straighten a dust-covered magazine. The mug next to it is half filled with something entirely too green and fuzzy for coffee. There's a phone with a rotary dial, like the kind you see in old movies, on a desk in the corner of the room. When I pick it up, there's no dial tone.

I try Mom's number.

Nothing.

"Aaron?" My voice is loud and shrill. Nothing. The rooms are empty, and the silence is too much for me.

Outside, the snow deepens.

Sometimes I wonder who they see when they visit me, Cor. Not Kyra. Not me. Because they've never seen me. Not even when I tried so hard for them to notice me, to get to know me. They see a girl who can help them, who will answer their requests and their petitions. (I can't call them prayers. How could I?)

But how can I deny them?

My art has worth to them. Even if it doesn't to me. They see it as otherworldly, meaningful.

If they need someone to believe in, how could I take that away from them? At least what I do now makes Lost a better place. It may not be the same as understanding legends and myths, but together, we're creating new stories.

It matters. I matter. I've never felt like this before.

How can I deny them?

I can do this, if it's the only thing I can do. Nothing else was enough.

I'll never tell them that I need something to believe in too.

UNEXPECTED FRIENDSHIP

I KEEP KYRA'S TATTERED NOTEBOOK CLOSE. I'VE SETTLED into one of the chairs near the fireplace again when a loud knock echoes through the entrance hall. I tense all over. *Who's here? Why is* anyone *here? What do they want?* Sheriff Flynn made it clear that Lost wants nothing to do with me, and I want nothing to do with it.

But what if... What if they refuse to let me leave? I have little in the way of defense. I could flee the spa, but I can't flee Lost until my plane arrives tomorrow.

I glance out a window and see Roshan and Sam standing outside, outfitted with backpacks and sleeping bags.

I open the door. "Hi?"

"Hi," Roshan says. We've only crossed paths a few times this week, but he smiles like we're old friends. "Can we come in?"

"Um, sure?" I step aside to let them to enter.

Roshan strides in, followed by Sam, who wraps me in a hug. He smells of woodsmoke, and the scent is so potent, so pungent, that I freeze. Immediately, he pulls back. He looks at my face, and realization washes over his. "I was burning waste," he says with a catch in his voice. "I promise you, I would never."

I manage to get my breathing under control. "I know," I say, although I don't. I really don't. "The smell—I can still taste the smoke. I still can't believe that fire..."

"That's why we're here," Roshan says. He tosses a sleeping bag on the floor. "After last night, you shouldn't be alone. With grief, you shouldn't be alone."

Sam nods. "I'm sorry. I should've changed."

"It's okay." I'm not sure what else to say. *Thanks? I appreciate your being here?* I like Roshan from what I know of him, and once upon a time, Sam was a friend. But so many of the people I used to trust have hurt me over the last few days, and I don't want to be caught off guard again. Besides, if they stood by and watched this happen to Kyra, I don't want to be their friend anyway.

Roshan looks around with a frown, then swings his backpack off his shoulder and places it in front of the fireplace. He starts to unpack what's inside—a loaf of bread. Cheese. M&M's. Two bottles of soda. More chocolate. Goldfish crackers. Pop-Tarts. He hums while he works, and I recognize the tune as a Christmas carol, not the terrifying melody I keep hearing from the rest of the town.

And despite myself, I laugh. "Are you preparing for a siege?"

"We didn't think you had time to eat—or a place to eat, for that matter," Sam says. "But Dad isn't much of a cook, and…"

"The rest of the town wasn't very generous," I finish for him.

"Fortunately, my father keeps our pantry well stocked," Sam says. He shrugs. "Dad was an Eagle Scout. We could've brought you gas, rope, and dried peas too, but that seemed a bit too 'end of the world.'"

A small part of me wants to challenge him that this is, in fact, the end of the world, but I know better. Especially when Roshan unwraps the cheese, and my mouth begins to water.

"I don't trust you," I say, honestly. "But since you come bearing food, I won't say no."

Sam looks crushed at that news, but Roshan nods. "I can work with that. And company?"

I glance around the spa. "I'm counting on you to keep the nightmares at bay."

I want him to laugh. I want to laugh too. But I can't. The words are true.

I pick up my parka from the floor and shrug into it. "I'll be at the springs."

....

I SIT AT THE EDGE OF THE HOT SPRINGS. I'M DRESSED warmly enough, and there's a weird temperature balance between the deep snow and the hot water. I don't know how much time has passed. Minutes? Maybe days or hours. Silence always seems to make time go slower. Loneliness too.

I smell the food before I hear the footsteps, and this time, my stomach actually groans.

But it isn't Roshan as I expected. It's Sam. He holds an old blanket from one of the upstairs bedrooms.

Sam hands me a cheese sandwich, the bread fresh and fragrant. I never thought a sandwich could look like food from the gods.

"If we had a fire here, we could grill it," he says.

I munch on the sandwich. "We could have s'mores." *Kyra and I made s'mores here, every summer.*

"Picnic around the fire, under the stars?"

"Don't go getting any romantic notions," I say. "Besides, it's still snowing."

Sam smiles. "Wouldn't dream of it."

"Don't take this the wrong way," I say after I've devoured a handful of Goldfish crackers, "but there were entire months where I don't think I heard you say a single word. It almost made me wonder if you could talk."

"I didn't feel like I had much to say. Not anything worth contributing to a conversation, at least." He shrugs—or winces, maybe. "Besides, it's much easier to observe in silence. When you don't draw attention to yourself, it's amazing how easily people forget that you exist."

I've heard those words before.

"Kyra used to say the same thing," I whisper.

The snow crunches and Roshan appears with more food. He sits next to Sam, close. "What are you talking about?"

"Invisibility," Sam says.

I shiver. I have so much to ask the two of them. Sam, who was here, the sheriff's son who learned to smile. Roshan, who didn't know *my* Lost, but must have seen how the town changed. But it feels so wrong to be here with them without Kyra, and I can't find the right words yet.

"How did you even find Lost, Roshan?" I ask instead. "It's not like Lost Creek is known outside of Alaska. Or outside of the town itself, even."

Roshan nibbles at a bit of cheese. "How much do you know about geology—or chemistry, for that matter? Because I can try to explain why the ground is rich here, but it can get pretty boring. The gist of it is, Father owns a company that produces tungsten alloys. He's been on the lookout for private mining opportunities, and he stumbled upon Lost. Between the mining history here, the temperature, and the geology of the earth's crust, he thought it would be the perfect place. Plus, there are fewer competitors here in the middle of nowhere than in, say, Russia or Canada. Though, of course, he has to consider the environmental impact and the local effect on Native communities. He wants to do this right, if there is such a way."

He's more matter-of-fact about the possible consequences than all of Lost has been. "How did he stumble upon it?" I wonder.

Roshan scratches his ear, a little self-consciously. "I've spent a lot of time traveling with Father during school holidays. From rainy old England to Dad's family in India to everywhere in the world. Alaska always sounded like the stuff of legends to me. I wanted an excuse to travel here, so I traced down the geological surveys and investigation reports."

"Is Lost everything you expected?" I try and fail to keep the bitterness out of my voice.

Roshan looks at Sam. "Yes, it is."

Sam smiles, and vague blotches of red appear on his cheeks. He peeks up at the overcast sky. "You know the town never meant for any harm to come to Kyra, don't you, Corey?"

I don't think they cared enough to consider harm. But even if they had… "I never meant for any harm to come to Kyra either, and yet here we are. Intent only takes us so far. It's a shield people hide behind but not a weapon." I sigh. "I'm glad you love it here though, Roshan. I did too. It was home to me."

"Not anymore?"

"Not anymore."

He squeezes my shoulder. "It's—"

He means it as a joke, but "Ye" I hug my knees close. "Sam— you came to seeKyra, didn't you?"

He smiles — a sad smile "otfor the paintings. She seemed lonely, and I was lonely. I red we could be lonely together. I regret not going to her a long time ago. But when you were here two you were inseparable. I didn't think you wanyone else to intrude. When you left… I didn't want be completely on her own."

"Was she… Whappy

He glances at the spa "Sometimes. But I think she wanted more life. She would've escaped if she could have."

As he says it something near the tree line catches my eye. The shadows outside the spa grounds are deep and dark, so I can't tell what it is. A tree bending in the wind? An animal perhaps? A person?

I squint, but can't be sure. Maybe I'm imagining

things. The lines between reality and the imaginary have blurred too much already.

"Corey?" Sam's voice draws me back.

"Hm, yes?"

"Do you remember Kyra's presentation about the stone labyrinths of Ihoi Zayatsky Island? I don't even remember what class was for, only that Kyra happened to be reading Russolkbre ad wanted to talk about mysteries rather than..."

"I remember." Je, though it feels... I remember that K Buso rem... people laughed at the presentation. (Maybe... Sam. Maybe this is history.) They already thought she was odd the entation further proved to them that she was.

But studying the nd just been about the school project. That k, as cycling back into depression, and unlike h, she couldn't turn to painting to cope. The... soothing, ideas that her mind could ponder... been curious about the labyrinths for month ar urrounding areas — Onega Bay and the Sol... ds — were high on her list... of places to visit. It th, talking about the labyrinths simply made it easier to function.

And eventually, she felt better again. Or at least, I thought she did.

I don't think they cared enough to consider harm. But even if they had... "I never meant for any harm to come to Kyra either, and yet here we are. Intent only takes us so far. It's a shield people hide behind, but not a weapon." I sigh. "I'm glad you love it here though, Roshan. I did too. It was home to me."

"Not anymore?"

"Not anymore."

He squeezes my shoulder. "Outsider."

He means it as a joke, but... "Yeah." I hug my knees close. "Sam? You came here to see Kyra, didn't you?"

He smiles a sad smile. "Not for the paintings. She seemed lonely, and I was lonely too. I figured we could be lonely together. I regret not having done that a long time ago. But when you were here, the two of you were inseparable. I didn't think you wanted anyone else to intrude. When you left... I didn't want her to be completely on her own."

"Was she... Was she happy?"

He glances back at the spa. "Sometimes. But I think she wanted more from life. She would've escaped if she could have."

As he says that, movement near the tree line catches my eye. The shadows outside the spa grounds are deep and dark, so I can't tell what it is. A tree bending in the wind? An animal, perhaps? A person?

I squint, but I can't be sure. Maybe I'm imagining

things. The lines between reality and the imaginary have blurred too much already.

"Corey?" Sam's voice draws me back.

"Hm, yes?"

"Do you remember Kyra's presentation about the stone labyrinths of Bolshoi Zayatsky Island? I don't even remember what class it was for, only that Kyra happened to be reading Russian folklore and wanted to talk about mysteries rather than explanations."

"I remember." I smile, even though it feels unnatural. I remember that Kyra. But I also remember how some people laughed at her poster presentation. (Maybe not Sam. Maybe this is revisionist history.) They already thought she was odd, and that presentation further proved to them that she was.

But studying the island hadn't just been about the school project. That week, Kyra was cycling back into depression, and unlike with her highs, she couldn't turn to painting to cope. The mysteries were soothing, ideas that her mind could ponder in loops. She'd been curious about the labyrinths for months, and the surrounding areas—Onega Bay and the Solovetsky Islands—were high on her list of places to visit. But that week, talking about the labyrinths simply made it easier for her to function.

And eventually, she felt better again. Or at least, I thought she did.

But right here and now, at this abandoned spa, I can't help but wonder about time and the death of stars. The stars we see in the night sky are so far away that it takes years for us to see it when they die. I can't help but wonder if Kyra had burned out long before I left—and if we simply hadn't seen it.

NORTHERN LIGHTS

HOME IS A THOUSAND SMALL DETAILS. THE FEEL OF plowed roads beneath my feet. The gardens protected against moose. The smell of the air when the snow clears. The brilliant colors in the night sky. The stars see everything, and I wish I could ask them my questions, but I know they won't answer.

Sam leans back on his elbows and stares up. "We get so used to these skies. It's easy to forget how beautiful and terrifying they are."

"Terrifying? Does the scale scare you?"

He shrugs. "The emptiness, mainly."

"But the heavens aren't empty," I say. "They're endless.

We live in this tiny corner of the universe, up against impossible odds. And yet, here we are. We're made of stardust. We're supernovas. We're entire constellations. That comforts me."

And when the first flames light up the sky, something inside me unclenches. And I *smile*.

Home is awe and wonder.

Home is the aurora borealis.

....

ONE YEAR BEFORE

"People have told stories about the stars since the dawn of time." Kyra wrapped her arms around her knees and kept her eyes trained on the heavens. "They told stories to make sense of these lights in the sky and of the shapes they made."

I lay back to take in the northern lights. With the warmth of enough blankets, the soft snow was surprisingly comfortable. I rested my head on my arms and stared at the spectacle above us. The aurora was red tonight. "We told stories before we knew better. We have science now. The constellations. The colors. We know now that what we're seeing is excited oxygen atoms."

"Excited? Are the atoms *really* excited? Maybe they're terrified," Kyra said, challenge in her voice. "Science is a form of storytelling too."

Two could play that game. "*Excited* is a technical term. When the sun's electrons hit Earth's atmosphere, they hit atoms. Depending on the type of atom and the altitude, the color changes. Excited oxygen at a high altitude appears red, but auroras that are entirely red are quite rare."

"Aren't red skies a harbinger of doom? I'm sure I read that somewhere."

I glare at her. "At a lower altitude, excited oxygen gives off a green glow—which also happens to be far more visible."

"Hm, let's see… Green skies must be a sign of prosperity. Or tornadoes."

Kyra knew exactly where my buttons were and how to push them. "When you reach lower altitudes, the particles are less likely to hit oxygen atoms and more likely to hit nitrogen. Nitrogen turns blue or purple. That's why the sky changes colors. It's science, not fortune-telling." I glared at her again, and I could feel her smile.

"It's a veritable rainbow of colors."

"Oh hush, you." I rolled my eyes. "Four colors. Not at all an entire rainbow."

"Poetic license."

"*Science*."

She didn't respond immediately, but as hints of green started to appear amid the red in the sky, she continued. "In Norse mythology, the gods built a bridge between their realm and the mortal world. Bifröst. A rainbow bridge. A *burning* rainbow bridge, according to some. What if this is what they meant?" She pointed to the arcing colors above us.

"Maybe it is, but you can't walk on light," I say. "Or breathe that high up in the atmosphere."

Kyra laughed. "My point is, if there were a bridge between earth and heaven, wouldn't it be magnificent?"

I relented. "Yes, it would."

She nodded. "This is it, I think. Our bridge from this piece of frozen wilderness to the rest of the world. From here, we can go everywhere."

....

As much as I know that the aurora borealis can be explained by science, I can't help but feel some of the magic that Kyra always saw. And tonight, that is the reassurance, the bridge I need, to ask the question that has been burning inside me.

"Sam?" I keep my voice down and glance at him sideways. "Did anyone try to help Kyra escape?"

Sam seems at a loss for words and, for a moment, he is the quiet boy I remember.

Then he shakes his head. "I wish we'd tried, but Kyra's father never would have let us. We all knew that Kyra's death was foretold."

DAY FIVE

THE SMELL OF
CHANGING WEATHER

NINE MONTHS BEFORE

"Close your eyes and clear your mind," Kyra told me. We sat on the steps of the spa. She had her arms wrapped around me as I leaned into her, and around us, the landscape was frosted, but we were warm.

I closed my eyes and focused on Kyra's presence. It had been a good day, but she was becoming restless again.

"Breathe in, slowly."

The smell of snow and ice was crisp, cold, and unyielding.

"Can you smell the difference?"

I tried again, then shook my head. "Do you think it'll storm again?"

"No."

"Then I don't know what you want me to notice," I said and tilted my head to look at her. "The air smells the same as it has all winter."

"There's an earthiness beneath the frost," she said with a hint of impatience. "It wasn't here a week ago, and it's getting stronger."

She pulled away from me and got to her feet, then started to walk toward the hot springs.

These were once natural springs, but when the spa was built, the swimming area was plated with concrete, which had gone green with age. It looked like an old swimming pool under a cover of mist.

In years past, the hot springs were said to be a source of natural healing, but few people used them these days—certainly not the people of Lost. The spa looked too dilapidated, although in the summer months, a few backpackers would occasionally set up camp nearby to take advantage of the springs.

I joined Kyra at the edge, looking out over the misting water. "Can you smell it here?" she asked.

"I can hardly smell *anything* but rotten eggs."

Kyra turned to me and instead of the frown I expected, she was smiling, radiantly. "It's the smell of hope, Cor.

It's the smell of earth and sunlight and life. The rivers will break up soon."

I stared at her. Breakup was the dawn of spring, the time when the ice on the rivers started showing cracks, when the snow melted, and when, for a while, Lost turned into the muddiest mess on earth. But spring was still weeks away.

I must have looked dubious, because she shrugged. "They will. The weather is changing. The birds are returning. I've seen buds in the trees. Spring is everywhere."

I wrapped my arms around her and squeezed tightly. "You know I always believe you."

"But?" She always heard the words I didn't speak.

I looked out over the springs again. We'd planned to go camping here this summer, before Mom decided to upend our lives and accept the job in Winnipeg. Spring may have been a sign of hope for Kyra, but I wanted to cling to winter, to here, to home, a little bit longer.

"It's too early in the year. The temperature is freezing. We barely have any daylight yet. I would love for spring to arrive, but we've never had such a short winter."

Kyra didn't seem fazed. "It'll happen. I promise you, it will," she said. "Trust me."

I nodded.

Two days later, the rivers broke up.

UNDERSTANDING DAWNS

WITHOUT MY PHONE, I DON'T KNOW WHAT TIME IT IS. Without daylight, it's even harder to tell. Bleary-eyed, I reach for my makeshift pillow and cling to it. It's morning. At least, I think it's morning. I replay what happened last night. Friendship. A fragile sort of community. And the drama of the night sky.

I *slept*. Not enough to make up for all the nights without rest, but enough to make me feel halfway human again, enough to make me feel more at ease.

I switch on the bedside lamp, and the calm I'd found shatters. The sleeping bag is covered with pink salmonberry blossoms. I scramble out of bed to put distance between me and them. These flowers weren't here last night. Someone spread them on top of me while I was sleeping, and I didn't even notice. *Sam? Roshan?*

Kyr—no. I can't keep hoping that she'll appear. And whoever this was, they could've taken my stuff, they could've hurt me. Or worse.

I snatch my clothes off of the portable radiator and slip into them. The warmth envelops me. I pull Kyra's letters from under my pillow and hug them close.

I head out to check on Roshan and Sam but come to an abrupt stop in their doorway.

I'd expected to find them in separate sleeping bags. Instead, they lie together on the raggedy bed. Roshan's arm hangs across Sam's shoulders, and their legs and the blanket are all tangled together. Sam snores softly.

As quietly as I can, I step back into the hallway. A floorboard creaks and Roshan shifts, but neither he nor Sam wakes.

So this is why the sheriff's son smiles.

I walk back to the main hall and sit down on the steps. Emotion I haven't felt in days courses through me. From the soles of my feet to the tips of my fingers, I feel *joy*. Pure, unadulterated joy. Still, even if some happiness comes out of these nightmarish few days and Kyra's last nightmarish months, it won't be worth it; nothing is worth the cost of Kyra's life. But that doesn't mean that this isn't *good*.

An old sorrow blooms in my chest. Regret. I wish I could've given her that same happiness. I wish I could've given her more than friendship. I know well enough neither of us would've been happy if we'd tried to change for each other. I know love isn't a magic medicine that can cure mental illness. But it might have treated her loneliness.

Still, I can't change who I am any more than she could've changed who she was. I wasn't in love with her, and as much as I wish I could've been, she deserved more than a lie. We both deserved to be true to each other.

And maybe I should've been more truthful more often.

I rake my fingers through my hair. Someone stumbles in the bedroom behind me. I rest my chin on my hands and stare out across the entry hall. I count the balusters. On the side of one, I find carved: *Kyra was here*. I trace the words carefully. I'd forgotten about that. We made these carvings, years ago. Kyra wanted to leave her mark, to prove that she'd been here, like others had done before us. On the railing upstairs, I'd carved my name too.

I hold on to the handrail, still remembering how her hands would trail the length of wood whenever we climbed these stairs.

Not much later, Roshan joins me. His hair is tousled, his shirt a mess of crumples. Worry lines his forehead when he looks at me, and I wince. He doesn't know what to expect from me—he can't know what to expect from me.

So I say, "Thank you for spending the night here. I managed to sleep soundly for the first time in days."

He nods.

And I say, "I want you to know that I'm happy for you and Sam." And that's the truth.

"Thank you," he says. His smile is soft and hesitant. "Kyra introduced us. We probably would've met sooner or later—Lost is certainly small enough—but I owe her that. What's more, she accepted us without question."

That same pang of regret flows through me. "She would."

He holds out another sketch. Roshan and Sam, all tangled together. Sam's arm hangs across Roshan's shoulders. They're in a different bed, but aside from that, it's the *exact* scene I just saw.

"I think I believed her, you know," he says. "Believed in her."

I clear my throat. I don't know how to respond to that. "Does your father—"

"My father knows," he says. "Sam's parents do too."

"And the rest of Lost?"

"Not yet. We're taking it slowly. Many people would be fine with us, but others… I'm an outsider. It's going to take time." He glances at me sideways, and I hear his unspoken question.

"I won't tell anyone," I promise. Besides, if Sheriff Flynn knows and approves, then the rest of the town will follow.

"Thank you."

"Kyra wrote about Lost's stories and Lost's secrets in her letters. It sounded so sinister, but—you were one of them, weren't you?"

He nods. "I have no idea if she drew us before she met me, or after, but…yeah."

Acceptance explains why he helped her, and why he believed in her, but it still leaves a sour taste in my mouth. At least it's a comfort to know that there was more to Kyra's legacy than death; there was love too.

TOP OF THE MORNING

TEN MONTHS BEFORE

KYRA AND I DROPPED BY THE POST OFFICE BEFORE SCHOOL to deliver some of Mom's outgoing mail. We were the first customers, and Mrs. Morden opened a new bag of cookies and offered us some. She had a smile for Kyra, but directed all her answers to me.

Some days, Kyra would roll her eyes at that. Today, she scowled. "I'm here too, you know."

She'd been in a mood when I stopped by her house to pick her up. She'd seemingly been awake all night painting, but all that was left were tattered shreds.

I'd picked up one of the larger pieces—a piece of a mountain landscape—but Kyra snatched it out of my hands before I could look at it closely. "Leave it. It's not important."

Clearly her mood hadn't improved.

Mrs. Morden's gaze focused on a point *past* Kyra. "I know, dear." And then she ushered us both toward the door. "The two of you should hurry. School's starting soon."

We were unceremoniously dumped on the sidewalk, where old Mr. Wilde passed us, muttering something about "the freak Henderson girl" before he pushed into the post office.

"Well, good morning to you too," Kyra shouted after him. Her anger sounded like a growl.

With a sigh, I hooked my arm through hers. "Don't mind them," I said. "They mean no harm."

Kyra pulled away from me. "I *do* mind them. I mind that they whisper about me. I mind that they won't look at me. Why *shouldn't* I mind them?"

"Because they don't know any better. They don't understand you."

"I've only lived here all my life. They *used* to know me."

"This is Lost. When Mrs. Lucas couldn't remember her grandchildren's names, your mom called her 'a little absentminded,' and Mrs. Morden took to writing the addresses on her letters when she forgot, rather than saying anything to her. We're good at pretending that nothing is wrong."

"You say that as if ignoring reality were a good thing."

"It's not, but it's not ill-intentioned, either. You're unpredictable, Kyr. But we know that you're more than the tricks of your brain."

"I know that," she snapped. "But sometimes I don't know if you do. You, this town—you love me *despite* my illness, while Lost hates me *because* of it. Did it ever occur to you that no one separates me from how my mind works? Love me or hate me if you want, I don't care. But do it for all that I am, with all that I am."

Her mouth was set and her hands were clenched into fists. On the other side of Main Street, people had stopped to stare and whisper at her outburst. And my cheeks felt hot. My vision swam. I didn't know what to say.

Kyra waited, briefly, for a response. "Whatever. I'll see you at school." She stomped away from me.

But before she reached the top of the street, Kyra slowed to a halt. Her shoulders sagged. She was waiting for me. I ran to catch up. She didn't say anything when I reached her side. She didn't acknowledge me. Anger was still etched in the tense lines on her face. But still, she waited. Because even when we fought, we were all we had. It was us against the world. And we walked into school together.

THE ART OF LIVING

I CAN BELIEVE LOST THOUGHT KYRA WAS MAGIC. I caught myself believing the same thing on many occasions. And I certainly have no other explanation for the garden. For Mr. Sarin arriving to invest in the mine, immediately after Kyra painted a prosperous town. For the drawing of Roshan and Sam together.

Or even for the painting that started it all, of a bird with a broken wing.

Maybe it was coincidence? Sometimes strange things happen, and we have no explanation. But what defies explanation for me is how none of them tried to save her. Not Sam, despite his proclamation of friendship.

Not any of the people who watched her grow up. Not even her parents.

Kyra's paintings changed Lost for the better. It's easy to see how happy Sam and Roshan are. Sam tells me that Mrs. Morden has taken to whistling while she works, and everyone who visits the post office is cheerier for it. People hold their heads high, and there seems to be a common understanding between them, even if I'm not part of it. They see each other and nod or grab hands in passing. They whisper stories about Kyra. About the stories she told. They share their own stories.

They have hope. They're happy.

Kyra would be proud to see this side of Lost, the changes she inspired. Kyra wanted to make the world a better place, and she started in Lost Creek. My Kyra was a wonderful, ordinary, lonely girl. Lost Creek's Kyra was the girl of legends and stardust.

And she died.

Even if Lost treated Kyra like an oracle, their faith was never worth Kyra's pain, her death. I don't understand why Lost's happiness didn't start with helping her. They owed her that. They owed her community. They owed her life.

But as much as the town believed in her, they still didn't value her enough to save her.

And I lost myself to the world outside the town's borders. I forgot about her too.

....

I walk back to Lost with Roshan and Sam. I would have stayed at the spa, but the Hendersons still have my passport and my flight is in twenty-four hours.

Before we cross the tree line, I linger. "You two should go ahead. It won't do either of you any favors to be seen with me." I don't want them to pay a price for their kindness.

"I don't think there's anyone left in town who doesn't know where we spent the night," Sam says softly. "Word travels fast here."

"Will you get in trouble with your dad?" Sheriff Flynn wouldn't let anyone harm Sam. They may not always see eye to eye, but the Flynns are fiercely protective of one another. And Roshan's father will soon be bankrolling the entire town.

"Nah. Kyra would've wanted us to help you."

Nevertheless.

"Please be careful," I tell them.

Roshan hesitates. "It may not be my place to say this, but before you leave, I think you should talk to the Hendersons. I know you've been avoiding each other. But they care about you, like a second daughter. You should sit down and talk."

I once considered the Hendersons my other parents. I thought they loved Kyra fiercely. That was before they let her die, and before they were willing to let me burn. "I'm honestly not sure if that's a good idea."

"Mr. Henderson's talking to our fathers again today, so I'm not sure if he'll be around. But Mrs. Henderson will be in the bakery. Go say goodbye. Don't leave on these terms."

My reply slips out before I can bite my tongue. "The only Henderson I want to talk to isn't here anymore."

STEALING IN

ROSHAN'S COMMENTS HELP ME CLEAR MY MIND. I WAIT until he and Sam are well out of sight, then head to the Hendersons'. If Mr. H is talking to Mr. Sarin and Sheriff Flynn, and Mrs. H is in the bakery, then the house will be empty, which is perfect.

I know where the keys are. Kyra and I crept through the house many times on missions to find food after our nightly escapades. Like two years ago, on the longest night, when we stayed out to watch the aurora borealis and completely forgot the time. Or last spring, when we scared each other telling ghost stories out by the hot springs. We were too terrified to walk back through the woods to Lost, so we spent the night in a bed at the spa, sneaking back into her house after the sunrise. The only difference is that now I don't *want* to be here. I double check that the street is empty, because I don't want the neighbors to alert the Hendersons if they see me, then I slip the key into the lock.

The house is quiet and dark. I pass the photos of Kyra, but I try not to look at them. I climb the stairs. My two best chances for finding my passport are in Mr. Henderson's study—a small office, opposite the master bedroom—or in the bedroom itself. Both were always strictly out-of-bounds for Kyra and me. I start with the study. But when I ease open the door, I gasp. Every inch of wall space is covered from floor to ceiling with bookshelves. I step closer to see what the books are. Unlike Kyra's room, the shelves aren't filled with stories. They're filled with books on mining and minerals. On the history of Alaska. On his father's research into the legends of the gold rush and the narrative history and current affairs of Alaska's Indigenous peoples. On the desk lies what looks like a blueprint of some sort, folded at the edges, and a historic map of Lost Creek.

I never knew that Mr. Henderson cared this deeply about Lost Creek. I glance again at the books on minerals. It might not be the town he cares about, but its riches. Around these parts, the gold rush is recent history and only a memory away.

I look over the shelves to see if my passport is lying

out before I turn to Mr. Henderson's desk. It's covered with stacks upon stacks of paper. Quotes from mining funds, in particular. I try not to shuffle the documents as I peek under them. Nothing.

The drawers. I feel a bit guilty going through those, but I need my passport back. I try not to read his letters as I leaf through to get to the bottom of the first drawer, and I ignore the checkbook in the middle drawer. *I shouldn't be here. I should take the mature route and go find Mr. H to ask him for my passport.*

It's just that I don't know if he'd let me leave. I don't know if he wants Kyra's story told. And I will tell it. The story of a lonely girl in an abandoned spa and the town who came to revere her. Though I don't think anyone will believe me. Even with Kyra's letters and her writing on the walls, who would trust our words—an outsider and a bipolar girl—over her father's word or the sheriff's?

But still, I need to try. I owe her that much, and so much more.

The third drawer holds office supplies: legal paper, envelopes, and pens.

My passport isn't here.

The front door opens and closes, and my heart slams into my throat. If Mr. Henderson finds me here, he'll kill me. I don't even know if that's an empty threat anymore. And it wouldn't be any better if Mrs. Henderson found me.

I slide into the hallway and close the office door behind me. On the landing, I avoid the creaky floorboards and slip around the bedroom door. Dim sunlight filters in through the window, and the deep blue bedspread glows.

Kyra once told me that there was a safe in here, and while I don't know the code, I have to try it. When I find the safe, I start with Kyra's birthday, then Lost's zip code.

I go through the most obvious choices, but nothing works. The safe mocks me with its refusal to budge.

Another door slams—somewhere inside the house. *The same person?* I shake my head and focus on the safe again.

I was convinced that Kyra's birthday would be the code, so I try it again. The lock doesn't click.

I try the date Kyra died.

It clicks.

The safe swings open.

My passport lies on top of a stack of papers.

I grab it and slip it into the pocket of my jeans. Then I still. Kyra's handwriting peeks out at me.

Corey

An envelope. Addressed to me. I pick it up as if the paper might burn me—or disintegrate at my touch. I don't trust simple appearances anymore. But the envelope is thick and weighty in my hands. The top has been carefully sliced open, and it's filled with folded papers.

My hands tremble and my heart pounds in my chest. I don't have time to look at these letters here, so I fold the envelope and slide it into my waistband. I close the safe and sneak across the bedroom and into the hall.

Someone clears their throat.

My heart stops. I forget to breathe. All I want is to disappear where I stand.

"What do you think you're doing?" Mrs. Henderson asks icily. She stands at the top of the stairs, flour from the bakery still dusting her clothes.

I haven't seen her since the night of the fire, and she doesn't even ask how I am. She doesn't soften. Mrs. H, who was almost as close to me as my own mother. She is a stranger now. And I'm terrified.

The passport and letters burn in my pocket.

"Corey. I asked you what you're doing here." Mrs. H's voice is flat.

"I came to see…" My voice wavers and those four words leave me out of breath. I try again. "The door was open. I came to see how you were—how you were doing."

"And when you didn't find me downstairs, you decided to wander around our house?"

I used to be at home here. I keep that to myself. I open and close my mouth, then aim for a half truth.

"My flight leaves tomorrow, and I needed my passport. I'd given it to Mr. H for safekeeping, so I came to ask for it. When I came in, I thought I heard a noise when I called, so I came up. I just… I wanted…" I'm rambling and I only stop when I run out of breath again. My cheeks feel red hot, so it must be obvious that I'm lying. Kyra used to tell me that I got too distracted by the details, and she was exasperated when I wanted to include them all.

"Your passport."

I wet my lips and nod.

Mrs. H glances from me to the bedroom and the cabinet that holds the safe. I can see her adding up the details. She shakes her head. "Run then. My daughter wouldn't have wanted you to stay here."

I push my hands into the pockets of my jeans, and my fingers curl around my passport. "I want to go home, Mrs. H."

"We take care of our own here, Corey. You wanted to lay bare our stories and share our secrets." Mrs. H tilts her head to the side, regarding me. "Then you have to be willing to pay the price for it."

I flinch. "Yes, ma'am."

"Leave while you still can. You're not welcome in my home anymore. You're not welcome in Lost anymore."

And with that, she steps aside to make room for me to pass her on the stairs. There is no warmth in her face.

There's nothing left of the kindness she'd showed count-less times, baking muffins for Kyra and me, telling stories about Kyra's grandfather and his escapades and travels, making tea and keeping me company on the days when Mom was at work and Kyra was ill.

She crosses her arms. "Leave, Corey. Now."

I go.

THE ART OF DYING

EXT. LOST CREEK—MAIN STREET—DUSK

Corey watches as Mr. Sarin and Sheriff Flynn walk along Main Street to the edge of town. They're deep in conversation. She can see their mouths move, but she can't hear them. It seems like they're always walking the same route whenever she sees them.

When Corey turns to go back to the spa, she is confronted by a group of Lost's students, fishermen, townspeople.

A mob. Piper leads the crowd.

Piper

Do you think you're so much better
than us? You come here all high and
mighty, tell us how we all misunder-
stood Kyra. Do you really think you
understood her better than we did?

*Corey steps back and hugs her arms
around her chest.*

Piper

We cared for Kyra. We fed her. We
clothed her. We listened to her. When
was the last time you listened to her,
really listened? We never asked her to
change. We never tried to fix her. We
accepted her.

Corey *(shaking her head)*:

Piper, you didn't acknowledge her
at all after her diagnosis. And when
you did, it was only because she could
be useful to you. You let her die. Don't

give me that nonsense about accepting
her. You didn't.

Piper steps forward.

Piper

We let her die? Do you even know
what you're talking about? She painted
her own death. That was what she wanted.
Do you know how much her visions meant
to us? She told the stories that gave
meaning to our lives.

Corey

She painted her own death, and you
didn't think that was a cry for help?
A sign that she was suicidal? Kyra was
ill, Piper.

Piper *(raising her voice in anger)*:

And she decided that it was her
time.

*Piper struggles to get her emotions
under control.*

Piper

Yes, she was ill, and that was all the more reason to let her go. You claim to have been her friend. Would you want her to be unhappy?

Corey *(stepping back at Piper's words)*:

Of course I didn't want her to be unhappy, but I didn't want her dead. She had a right to live. To fight. To feel, happiness and heartbreak. It. Wasn't. Her. Time.

Corey balls her fists and flinches at the pain radiating from her palm. She's grown deadly pale. Her fingers itch to hit something, but she restrains herself.

Corey

How dare you. How dare you deny Kyra a chance to live?
(whispering)
How dare we?

Piper

You scorn her when you scorn us.
Go home, Corey. Forget. It's best for
us all.

*Piper and the crowd take a step forward
together. They repeat the same words
Piper has spoken, in a violent, angry
mutter.*

Crowd

Go home. Forget.
Go home. Forget.

*They all step forward, moving as one,
their eyes trained on Corey. Slowly, they
begin to spread out.*

Crowd

Go home. Forget.
It's best for us all.

*They start to circle and close in.
Corey bolts.*

LETTER FROM KYRA TO COREY
UNSENT

Some days, I'm alone in this spa. Some days, there's an endless stream of people. Some days, I have friends. Sam smuggles me articles about current events from the school library, but that's all he dares to do. Aaron comes to check up on me every evening. He sends my letters. At least, I think he does. I have no way to know for sure. Maybe you never got any of them...

I tried to go for a run in the woods last night, but Dad brought me back here. He says he wants to keep me safe. He doesn't believe me when I tell him that I don't feel safe here. How could I? They're burning me up with all of the painting. I want to see Rowanne. I want to be able to sleep.

I want people to care about me, <u>not</u> in spite of my illness and <u>not</u> because of it. Because of <u>me</u>, Cor. Just because of me.

THE MIST, THE WOODS, THE DARKNESS

My PULSE RACES. My HEART POUNDS. I PUSH MY HANDS against my temples and bolt.

Get away. Get out. Run, Corey.

I head into the woods.

We've lived through the longest night, but the days are still darkened by shadows, mournful and deep. The forest is quiet, all sounds dampened by the snow, even the snap of branches I push out of my way and the crunch of snow beneath my feet. Everything is softer here.

I won't hear anyone following me.

I scramble toward the place where the woods should

clear around the hot springs—only to be met with a dead end. I blink. Turn. More trees.

My heart skips, and I have to force myself to keep breathing.

I try to retrace my steps, but the path behind me has disappeared under a new layer of snow. The light trickles away and night creeps in. *Where am I?* I've never seen this part of the woods before. It's as if the trees have circled me. I can't move. I'm lost. I'm *lost*.

I'll never get out.

The absence of direct sunlight makes the air colder, and when I breathe in, I taste snow. The air is a fine mist.

I run. I don't know where I'm going. I don't know what I'm doing. *I have to get out.* I can hardly see with the pines above me and the clouds covering the moon. The cold air scorches my lungs, and I double over and clutch my stomach.

I sprint again. I stumble and trip, hitting the snow hard. Pain shoots through my shin, while the cold seeps through my pants and crawls up my spine.

I could die like this. Running into the woods, never to be seen again.

I scramble to my feet, despite my uneven footing. Sweat gathers at the back of my neck and turns to ice. I keep walking because I have to keep moving, I have to trust my instincts. If I stop, I will freeze. But I slow down my pace.

Step by step, I backtrack. I push my nails into the palm of my unharmed hand and try to clear my mind. *Focus.* I follow my own footprints. I keep an eye out for broken branches where I pushed through the foliage. I have to get back to the path—and move onward from there.

Finally, after what feels like an eternity, I stumble into a clearing. *Aaron's cabin.*

A plume of smoke rises from the chimney, and the lights are on inside.

KYRA VS. THE REST
OF THE WORLD

"AARON?" LIKE YESTERDAY, I KNOCK AND ENTER THE cabin slowly, but today I'm met with the comforting warmth of a fire. Aaron has the radio tuned to a classical station, and he sits at the kitchen table, working on his miniature plane.

He's so focused on applying the wheels to the landing gear that I don't think he hears me.

I clear my throat.

Aaron startles, scattering pieces of the plane across the table. "Corey! What are you doing here?"

"I…" I'm not sure what to say. "I came to see you yesterday, but you weren't here. You—this cabin"—I gesture around me—"it looked abandoned."

He frowns. "What are you talking about?" He looks around the room, as if trying to see what I'd seen. Everything is as it was yesterday, including his mug on the coffee table, but now his cabin looks lived in, homey.

I blink and shake my head. "I—I'm leaving early tomorrow morning. I wanted to say goodbye."

He scratches his neck. "Oh. Okay."

I try to find the right words. "I also wanted to ask… How did Kyra die? I promise, I won't hurt Kyra's memory. I don't want to get between Lost and its beliefs. But I need closure. She was my *best friend*."

This part of Kyra's story is still hazy to me. I know the Hendersons withheld Kyra's medication. I know the town believed that Kyra's death was foretold, so they didn't help her, even though she seemed to be suicidal. I know she was exhausted. But Kyra had also promised to wait. She knew I was coming.

"You saw her every day. You cared for her. You must know what happened." Aaron is silent, so I continue. "I know you know this isn't right."

His silence lengthens until, eventually, I sigh and stalk toward the door.

"Corey." Aaron's voice is quiet, and I have to strain to hear him over the radio. "Wait."

I bite my lip and perch against the kitchen counter. Aaron gets up and pulls a mug from a shelf, filling it with coffee from the pot. When he turns back to me, he has a haunted look in his eyes.

"Kyra had had enough of it," he says, without preamble. "She wanted out. She wanted to go to Fairbanks, to find that therapist of hers—Rowanne. She wanted to admit herself into a treatment center. Life here... It was devouring her. In that sense, Mrs. Henderson was right. She was burning up."

He holds out the mug to me, and I wrap my fingers around the hot ceramic. "What happened?"

Aaron rubs his ear. "You have to understand, Lost Creek had become a better place these last few months. Whether it was prophecy or not, Kyra's art brought us all together, and that, along with Mr. Sarin's potential investments, gave this town hope again. After so many years of struggling to make ends meet, hope can be a dangerous thing. They wanted to cling to it with both hands."

"Aaron. Tell me."

"She tried to get away. She said she was going to hitch a ride on the mail plane. She had a bag packed and everything, and she told me that she was going to get in touch with you as soon as she reached Fairbanks. She trusted you. She knew you would've understood her leaving."

She trusted me. The words pack a vicious punch. I don't know if I deserved her trust.

"What *happened?*" I ask, fiercer than I intend. "Did you tell anyone about her plan?"

Aaron recoils. "No! No, of course not. But it's hard to keep secrets in this community, you know that. Maybe she asked old Mrs. Morden for help too. All I know is I followed her into town to make sure she was safe. But when she made it to the airstrip to meet the mail plane, the town was waiting. And they refused to let her go. The sheriff. Her parents. Mr. Lucas. They turned her around, quick as that. Her father brought her back to the spa. I stayed far enough away that I couldn't hear what was said between them, but I could tell that they were arguing.

"When her dad left, Kyra locked herself in her room and didn't come out until much later that night, after I urged her to eat some food." He clears his throat. "She looked like she'd been crying for hours, but she smiled at me and ate every last morsel. Later that night, when I was out for my walk, I saw her sitting on the balcony, staring up at the stars. The Milky Way was so bright that night. It almost looked like she could step out onto it, like a road of stars into the heavens."

"And then?" The radio reception fades, and soft white noise fills the space between us.

Aaron grimaces, then continues. "The following night, I went to check on Kyra and she was gone. From her footprints, I thought maybe she had headed for the highway, so I went after her. She would have frozen before she saw a car, let alone reached the next town. But as I was walking, I noticed that the path to White Wolf Lake was trampled, like the whole town had trekked out there. So I went too. They must have followed Kyra out there, or maybe they pushed her out there, I don't know. Everyone was standing on the shoreline. The Hendersons. The sheriff. Mrs. Morden and her granddaughter, Piper. Everyone."

He pauses. "The moon was bright that night, but it took me a moment to see Kyra. She wasn't in the crowd—she was running across the ice. And she slipped. She fell. I don't know if the ice was weak or broken, but when she tried to get up, she fell through. I tried to push through the crowd, but no one moved to help her or make a path. They watched. They just watched."

His voice breaks. "She was too far away. In the time it took me to get to her, she was gone. There was nothing I could do to help her."

I close my eyes and see the townspeople standing around the burning cabin. The empty stares. Mr. Henderson clutching Kyra's scarf.

"They let her die," I whisper.

Aaron shakes his head. "She wanted to get out, one way or another. But Lost wanted to protect her legacy. They wanted to fulfill her prophecies. They needed to keep believing."

"She could've waited until I... I would've helped..."
My voice catches and I can't vocalize the rest of the
sentence. If I do, I'll start crying. And if I start crying, I'll
never stop.

Aaron puts an arm around me and speaks softly. "She
waited for a long time, but I don't think she could wait
any longer. Trust me, kid, I wish she were here too."

"They *killed* her," I choke.

"They didn't understand her. They were frightened of
her. They used her. *That's* what killed her."

Dear Corey,

I'm not sure if you'll ever read this, but I have to leave a note in case you come here and I'm gone, whatever gone means. I hope it means that I make it out of here alive, but if not... I still can't stay.

And if you do read this...

You were my best friend. For so long, you were my only friend. I never said thank you for that. I know I wasn't always the easiest person to be around. I know I pushed you away. I know you suffered for being my friend, though I hope it doesn't feel that way.

You made my life better by being in it.

We shared so much, happiness and anger, secrets and a kiss... But it's so hard to share fear. I tried to explain, but I knew you wouldn't understand. I don't think you could've. I know you thought I was fearless, but I never was. Until Lost discovered my paintings. And I forgot to be afraid. Those first days, those first weeks, when they kept coming to me, I thought maybe Lost had actually changed for the better. I forgot to be afraid.

But I am now. And I should have been when you left.

I lost you. I don't know if I lost you when you left or before then. There was so much we didn't talk about. Like those times we hurt each other and pretended later that nothing had happened.

I know I scared you, and that's one of the reasons why I kept silent about everything I felt. I didn't want you to try to fix me. I struggled. I still do. Sometimes the days, the nights feel endless.

But I've also been happy. Unconditionally, intensely happy. And I don't think anyone ever understood that. Not even you.

I'm tired, Cor. I don't want to be stuck here. I miss you more than I thought was possible. We should have tried harder. We both should have tried harder.

I'm tired. I'm so tired.

I hope this feeling will pass, I hope this day will pass and the night will come.

I want to see you. I still want to travel. I still want to see the world and hear its stories. I need to leave Lost.

I hope this pain will pass.

But if I'm honest, I don't think it will. Not this time.

I know I promised I would wait for you. Please believe me when I tell you I tried. I tried for so long.

I have nothing left here. I need to find my own path.

No matter where you are, a piece of my heart is yours. No matter where I am, part of me will always be waiting for you.

I turn the page, but I've reached the end of Kyra's writing. I hold the envelope upside down. A smaller piece of paper slips out and drifts onto the balcony. It's a black-and-white sketch of the aurora borealis, stars falling to earth. And Kyra and I, standing together, hand in hand, looking up at the sky.

BELONGING

FIVE MONTHS BEFORE

I PUT MY PEN ON THE PAPER AND STARED AT THE blank sheet.

Dear Kyra.

What can I tell you? I'm happier here at St. James. I didn't think I would be, but I am.

Lost Creek was a bubble, an almost all-white, conservative town with little room for wayward girls. Compared to Lost, St. James was a revelation. There were more students here than there were people in Lost, and far more perspectives on the world. To me, St. James was a constellation. To Kyra, it would've been a whole mythology of stories.

But how could I tell her that while she was stuck in Lost? How could I tell her that Eileen wanted to write books? That Noa read superhero stories? That there was an entire library with shelf after shelf of histories and myths and legends? I couldn't tell her that she belonged here—and taunt her with my happiness.

"Cor?" Noa's voice echoed through the hallway. "Practice starts in ten. You ready?"

"Coming!" I pushed the piece of paper under my books and dumped my pen in the drawer. *How can I tell her that this is where we're both meant to be, when only I can be here?*

I told myself I'd go back to the letter later. I never did.

BRUSHSTROKES

THERE IS LITTLE LEFT FOR ME TO DO IN LOST BUT TO count the hours until morning, when a plane will take me to Fairbanks. *Not everything is as it seems here*, the pilot told me when he dropped me off. He was right. Nothing was as it seemed here—nor as I remembered.

I read Kyra's last letter until I know it by heart. I leaf through her notebook again. So much is missing. There's a jagged seam down the spine where Kyra ripped out the first letters she sent to me. But there are more torn-out pages than letters I received. What did she write on those pages? Were they letters she intended to send? Or notes she made for herself? Sketches she shared with her visitors? I'll never know, and that makes me feel empty. How many notebooks could we have filled for each other if we'd tried?

I fold her last drawing and keep it safe in my pocket.

Lost doesn't want Kyra's words to venture beyond its borders. After all, it's easier to believe in legends than in truth, and her story was carefully cultivated. I will take with me what I can. I will protect her stories.

But I wish I could do more. My hands tremble with anger.

I would burn down this spa, like Lost burned down my house and Kyra's cabin. I would erase what Lost turned Kyra into and remind them all that Kyra's art was never as important as she was. But there is already so little left to hold Kyra's memory. If I torched this place, what would be left to bear witness to her? All I'd do is cause more destruction.

And Kyra would hate me for it. Not only because the spa shaped Lost Creek, but because it holds so many stories. This building holds a history richer than the life of one person, even if that person was my best friend. I can't touch that. I won't touch that. But oh, how I wish I could.

Instead, I find some of her paint brushes in her room. I cannot create like she did. I cannot tell stories. But I can retell her stories.

So for the next few hours, I stand on a chair, and I use the darkest green paint to write on the walls in the entrance hall. My brushstrokes begin shakily, the letters not always clear. But Kyra's voice is clear in my mind, and that's all that matters.

LET ME TELL YOU A STORY.

THERE ONCE WAS A GIRL WHO LIVED AMONG CANDLES AND FLOWERS AND OFFERINGS. SHE DID NOT BELONG IN THE WORLD AROUND HER, BUT SHE BELONGED TO THE WORLD. AND WHEN SHE TRIED TO CARVE OUT HER OWN SPACE, THE PEOPLE CAME TO HER, FOR SHE KNEW THEIR STORIES AND THEIR SECRETS.

THERE ONCE WAS A GIRL WHO WAS LONELY. BECAUSE THE PEOPLE WHO SOUGHT HER OUT WOULD INEVITABLY LEAVE WITH EVERYTHING SHE HAD TO GIVE THEM: HER HOPE AND LOVE AND PROMISES.

THERE ONCE WAS A GIRL WHO WAS ABANDONED. THESE PEOPLE GAVE HER WORTH, BUT THEY USED HER, DRAINED HER DRY, UNTIL SHE HAD NOTHING LEFT TO GIVE. AND THEN THEY DESERTED HER.

AND THE GIRL, WHO NEEDED SOMETHING TO BELIEVE IN TOO, WAS LEFT WITH NOTHING.

LET ME TELL YOU A STORY

SEVEN MONTHS BEFORE

ONCE UPON A TIME, TWO GIRLS SAT ON THE ROOF, watching the stars appear in the dim night sky. They each held bottles of lemonade, bars of chocolate, and unspoken questions.

I was counting down the days until our big move to Winnipeg, and we'd crossed into single digits. I didn't want to go. Kyra and I had so many plans, and the closer it came to my leaving, the more it felt as if I would be abandoning her, even if we stayed in touch. I was terrified our friendship would change. That we wouldn't remember everything we'd been to each other. That the time we'd spent together hadn't been enough.

"Do you ever wonder about that day in the garden?" I asked softly. It had been a long time since that awkward kiss, a long time since I'd tried to fall in love with Kyra, and a long time since she had fallen out of love with me. But I needed to know if she accepted me. "Would it be easier if I were attracted to you?"

Kyra took a sip of her lemonade and stared at the sky. It wasn't quite summer yet, but the nights had been growing increasingly short and light. We wouldn't see bright stars for months.

"Easier? Maybe. Better? No. You are who you are, Cor, and I am who I am. I wouldn't want either of us to change to be someone we're not. We'd hate each other for it in the end."

"I know."

"Then why ask?"

"Because..." I swallowed hard. I believed what I'd told her. That what mattered between us was our friendship. I'd seen other people's crushes fizzle out, but our friendship had held strong. But soon there'd be nearly three thousand miles between us, and I didn't know if friendship could survive that. "I'll miss you."

"I know. I'll miss you too, but we'll keep in touch. I'll write. I promise."

"When I come back during winter break, what will we do?"

Kyra leaned back and rested her head against my shoulder. We fit together, as if we were two pieces of the same puzzle. "We'll stay up all night and talk until the sun rises. We'll hike in the woods and tell each other scary stories. We'll go ice skating on White Wolf Lake. We'll have seven months to catch up on, and we'll do everything."

"Together?"

"Together."

STOLEN TIME

I SIT AT THE EDGE OF THE HOT SPRINGS. THE STEAM FROM the water forms clouds around me, and while it doesn't exactly keep me warm, it helps me not notice the cold. Or anything else, for that matter.

I loved this place, and I still do. These forests and hot springs are part of who I am. I will miss the summer nights when sleep eluded me because the sky was too bright. I will miss the air here, both the sulfur smell of the hot springs and the cold, clean air of the surrounding hills.

I will miss the Arctic. Kyra and I never did go to the Gates of the Arctic National Park, despite talking about it forever. I may not be as adventurous as Kyra was, but

I would have loved climbing to a summit to stand on the roof of our world.

I will miss being one of the only students in Lost to ever take an interest in physics; I remember how much that had pleasantly surprised our teacher. I will miss when we—all of Lost's students, Kyra, Piper, and Sam included—would have class on the shore of the lake when the weather finally turned warm, and the nights when we sat around a campfire, eating marshmallows until our jaws hurt.

I will miss our raggedy old house and my room, where I mapped the winter constellations on my ceiling with glow-in-the-dark stars. And Kyra's little cabin with super-heroes covering her door. And the little world we created for ourselves inside the small world of Lost, which was so separate from the overwhelmingly large world beyond.

But we were never quite safe there—and it wasn't only the rest of Lost that judged Kyra. It was me too. I thought I was a good friend to her, the best friend I could be. I thought life as we knew it was truth, instead of just another story we told. But maybe I never stopped telling stories either.

....

Kyra always said we all lived on stolen land. That this piece of Alaska was never rightfully ours. I never understood when she spoke of stolen land and stolen time.

I do now.

I will miss Lost. But I am taking my memories of Kyra with me—her laugh and the taste of her kiss and the warmth of her smile—and home will no longer be tied to this place.

THE WAY THE WORLD ENDS

"COREY? COREY, WHERE ARE YOU?"

For a single, perfect moment, I'm convinced it's Kyra calling me from beyond the springs. I answer as if it were. "Usual spot." And my heart shatters.

"Corey?" The voice sounds distant, and around me the landscape is still. There's no one here but a memory.

I wrap my arms around my knees. I want to go to Mom and Luke.

I close my eyes and imagine Kyra appearing in the mist of the springs. I can almost see it. Her hair would be mussed and her glasses would be lovely fog. She would settle next to me, take off her glasses, and clean them with the sleeve of her shirt, sticking out from under her parka.

I'd reach out and squeeze her hand.

You're here, I'd say.

I'm here, she'd answer.

You promised to wait.

I tried.

I promised to come home to you. I should have come sooner. I promised to remember us. I forgot.

Yes.

Forgive me.

But the fog obscures even this comfort from me. And a chill climbs up my spine. It's still too quiet.

Then comes her whisper. *What's wrong?*

I shake my head. *I don't know.*

The mist shifts and the shadows part. And Mr. Henderson stands in front of me, fury carved on his face.

....

Mr. Henderson towers over me. He's always been a man of few words, a stoicism not shared by anyone else in the family, but his body speaks volumes now, as rage burns in his eyes and anger pulses along his jaw.

"I want my daughter's possessions back, Corey."

I scramble to my feet and step away from the hot spring.

"You took a letter. You have no right to it. You have

no right to ruin her words. You stole it. I could have you arrested for theft."

"You stole her letters from her. From *me*. She didn't want you to have them."

Mr. Henderson takes another step closer and I take another step back.

"You were a good girl, Corey, but I won't let you ruin my daughter's legacy and run off with her memory. You do not understand how much Kyra mattered to Lost."

"Kyra was my best friend. I knew she mattered. You, on the other hand, never understood."

He lunges at me. I dodge as he reaches out to tackle me. Then I push. I'm not strong enough to floor him, but I throw him off balance for a moment. And I run.

His footsteps pound close behind me, but I don't look back. I dash into the building to take a shortcut to the woods.

Inside, the entrance hall is unnaturally empty as I sprint through it. My bag is upstairs, but I don't have time to grab it. I have Kyra's notebook and her letters and my passport. That's all that matters right now.

I race down the spa's service stairs and toward the kitchen. If I can get out through the window, I'll have a clear escape through the woods, rather than being cornered by the springs. Mr. Henderson will never find me in the darkness, between the trees.

I climb onto the counter and start to slide through the window when the shadows move again.

There's a reason I didn't hear his footsteps in the house.

Mr. Henderson is here, waiting for me.

ENDLESS NIGHT

I FREEZE. A CLOUD PASSES IN FRONT OF THE MOON AND we're thrown into darkness.

Mr. Henderson snarls. "You can't outrun me, Corey. You have nowhere to go. Hand over Kyra's letter, and you won't get hurt. Kyra was my daughter, and her legacy belongs to me."

Kyra's carefully crafted legacy.

"You have no right to it," I say.

"This is Lost's story, and we'll tell it the way we see fit. She wanted to be here. She belonged here."

I'm trapped. My hand inches to the pocket that holds her notebook and letter. "You let her *die*."

Mr. Henderson's smile turns into a grimace. "We fulfilled her prophecy."

Suddenly, someone rushes past me. Roshan launches himself at Mr. Henderson. They connect with an audible thud, and the momentum lands them both in the snow. Mr. Henderson's large hands clamp down on Roshan's arms.

"Don't! Kyra wouldn't have wanted this," Roshan pants. He holds on to Mr. Henderson and tries to wrestle him. Roshan is lanky and wired, but Mr. Henderson is bigger and stronger. He may not have Roshan's flexibility, but he has more endurance and he is terrifyingly determined. "Kyra cared about Corey. She loved her. She wouldn't want us to fight over some letters, not after everything she gave to Lost."

"Corey is not a part of our community," Mr. Henderson seethes. "She's an outsider."

"She was Kyra's best friend," Roshan says as I shout, "I'm not an outsider!"

I start forward to help Roshan.

His gaze snaps toward me and he shakes his head. Mr. Henderson uses the opportunity to push Roshan off him. Roshan gasps, but quickly gets back on his feet.

"Corey, go!" His shout sets me in motion. Before I can see if Roshan manages to grab hold of Mr. Henderson again, I jump off the window ledge and into the snow. I head straight for the darkness of the trees.

ENDLESS DAY

I RUN INTO THE DARK, DARK WOODS. DEEPER AND farther than I've gone before. I have to get away.

I know I'm being followed. This forest has eyes. The trees are watching me. The wildlife is watching me. It's dangerous here, but it's far more dangerous at the spa and in town.

He'll never let me leave.

I run until my legs become too heavy to lift and my sides ache. The ground slopes up. The moonlight doesn't filter through the trees anymore. The snow is loose and tugging me down.

Endless night.

He's coming for me.

I stumble and get back up.

I can't see where I'm going.

Even my arms are heavy now.

Followed. Hunted. Terrified.

My lungs burn like they'll burst. I stumble into a small clearing and drop to my hands and knees. I gulp in the frosty air.

The world spins around me.

The moonlight reflects off the snow, and it's as bright as the stars above, as bright as almost-day.

Endless day.

I don't know where I am. This secret corner of the world. If I died here, no one would find me for weeks.

Someone hums—or is it the wind?

My vision turns upside down and I cough. Retch. Tears burn my eyes and my head pounds.

I drop to the ground and roll onto my back. My breath comes in heaves. I pat my pocket to make sure Kyra's notebook is still there. At least I'm not alone.

No human will find me, but the wolves will. In that, I feel almost safe. I breathe. And find my peace in the stars.

But a noise grows. Crunching. Swooshing. And Mr. Henderson comes crashing into the clearing with a dangerous hunger in his eyes and blood on his hands.

Come to steal your soul away.

COME TO STEAL
YOUR SOUL AWAY

I SCRAMBLE TO MY FEET AND SCREAM. MY VOICE CARRIES, but there is no one except the two of us to hear it.

Mr. Henderson advances on me.

"You don't have to do this," I say. "They're just letters. I'll leave in the morning. I won't be a threat to you anymore."

"You've always been a threat to us. To Kyra. You distracted her from her true purpose." Mr. Henderson corners me, and all that's left of him is anger—or maybe despair.

"Mr. H. *Please*."

This man used to carry Kyra and me on his shoulders.

He would find ways to talk to Kyra when no one else could, not even me. He would be away for weeks at a time, tending to his investments, but when he was home, he anchored Kyra's world. She trusted him, and so did I.

I try to crawl away, but he's taller, stronger, faster.

His hands clamp around my throat and I can't breathe I can't breathe I can't breathe. I twist and claw and kick, the barely healed cuts from two nights ago opening up again, but Mr. Henderson does not relent.

"No one will come looking for you here," he says softly, increasing the pressure. Shadows creep into the edges of my vision. "I'll make it look like an accident. It's not difficult, you know. Plenty of places here where a girl could fall in the darkness. You could drown in the lake, and no one would be the wiser. They say it's a peaceful death, drowning."

I ram my knee upward and he hisses when it connects with his groin. He stumbles, but he doesn't let go.

I can't breathe.

"You know, if your body were never found, there would be no crime. A tragic accident, at most. Plenty of animals roam these woods, even in the dead of winter. You would be nothing more than prey. Easy dinner for the wolves. And I'm sure they would appreciate it."

My vision goes black.

"No one comes between me and my daughter."

And then I fade away.

SAVING THE WORLD

I DON'T SEE MY LIFE FLASH BEFORE MY EYES. I DON'T SEE stars. I don't feel panic. What builds inside me is an unwavering determination. I refuse to accept this as the end.

I. Refuse. To. Die.

I arch back in the snow, and going on pure fear, I lash out again. I claw at Mr. Henderson's face and at his hands. I kick him again, *hard*. My knee connects with his groin once more, and this time, he lets go.

He curses, his voice raw.

I drink in sweet, pure air. Everything hurts, breathing most of all. But I can't soothe the pain or allow myself to give into it. I have to move.

My eyes water and I scramble to put distance between us. I try to get to my feet, but my vision twists. I crawl.

Mr. Henderson's hand closes around my ankle. I open my mouth to scream—but all I manage is a dry sob.

"Leave me alone."

"No."

I turn to face him and *stop*.

With one hand, Mr. Henderson holds my foot. With the other, he holds a knife. I recognize it from their kitchen. A boning knife, a carving knife, a chef's knife.

He holds the knife just above my bunny boot. If he pushes any harder, it'll slide through fabric, skin, muscle. If I can't stand or walk, I'll freeze to death here.

Oh God, he's going to kill me. He's really going to kill me. I can't escape.

"I didn't want to do this, Corey," he says slowly. "But I cannot let you leave. And blood will bring out the hunters."

Kyra used to tell me fables about wayward girls who wander into the woods and are dragged off by wolves, never to be seen again. They're cautionary tales. But wolf attacks do happen, and Mr. Henderson wouldn't even have to kill me himself. Leaving me wounded and bleeding would be enough.

He traces the knife along the rim of my boot and I freeze midkick. I'm trapped.

"Give me the letter, Corey."

A cloud passes over the moon, casting us into darkness. I claw at the snow. It gives me no traction.

I lean into my anger instead.

"She didn't need you to protect her legacy. She needed you to protect *her*. Kyra. Her dreams. Her plans. Her future." Antagonizing Mr. Henderson while he holds a knife is certain self-destruction. But I couldn't stop if I wanted to. "She needed you to be her *father*."

He draws breath as if to speak, but I push on.

"Do you even know what painting meant to her? It was her coping mechanism, not her passion. She needed therapy. She needed medication. She needed help. She deserved acceptance. Neither of us gave her that."

The words hit a nerve. The knife eases against my skin.

"You don't understand anything," he snaps.

"I understand enough."

My fingers touch the notebook. The letter Mr. Henderson wants is inside it, and I won't be able to withdraw it without his seeing the notebook too. I don't *want* him to see it. Kyra didn't want him to have it. She hid it away for a reason.

But Kyra wouldn't have wanted this either. He won't listen to me. But maybe he'll listen to her. One day. Maybe if he reads her letter—*all* her letters—he'll understand her.

And maybe he won't. But if I take Kyra's notebook to the outside world, who would they believe? The words of a young, bipolar girl, or the collective testimony of an entire town?

Forgive me, Kyr.

"Mr. Henderson," I say.

His eyes flash. Once, I thought Kyra had her father's eyes. They both shared the same sharp intelligence and curiosity. But now he towers over me and hatred twists his features into harsh angles. He is nothing like Kyra anymore.

And I *pity* him.

I hold out the notebook for him to see, and he freezes. "Take her *letters*." Then I send it sailing through the air, as if it were a Frisbee, toward the edge of the clearing. In the shadows. If he doesn't find it soon, it'll likely be lost forever.

"Catch."

The instant he lets go of my leg, I scramble to my feet and run. Down the hill. Through the trees. Stumbling over the snow and the rotting branches beneath it. I run until I reach the spa, my leg aching and my eyes burning with tears.

Roshan catches me. There's a gash across his temple, but aside from that, he looks no worse for wear.

I nearly sob in relief.

"He needs me. He needs my father's investment. He would never have hurt me." Roshan is probably trying to make me feel better, but he doesn't. He holds out my backpack and what's left of my belongings. I don't have the energy to reach for it. I can't hold myself up. I can't keep my emotions at bay. I can't stop shaking.

I collapse onto the ground. Roshan kneels next to me and wraps an arm around me. "I'm here," he says. "I'll stay with you."

"I want to go home."

"I know."

Roshan shelters me from everything I'm afraid of as I cry myself dry. And when I stop shivering, he hugs me tighter.

"Kyra told me that you want to be an astronomer. The sky is clearing. Will you tell me about it?"

I bite my lip and glance up. I can see Venus from here, bright in the path of the moon. Gemini and Orion with Betelgeuse, high above us. Canis Major, and a muted Milky Way passing through. The sky around us edges blue, and a single meteor streaks down in a bright flash.

I smile.

Maybe this is why I never minded the night sky, even when I hated the darkness. Because there's so much light here.

DAY SIX

HERO DAYS

ALMOST TWO YEARS BEFORE

"Why do you call them hero days?" I asked Kyra early one morning. We'd walked out to the airstrip to see the sun rise above the mountains in the distance. It wasn't too long after the ice broke up, and sunlight felt like a luxury.

"Because every story needs a hero," Kyra said. "And I would like to be the hero of my story."

"Can I be your sidekick?"

"I'd rather you be the hero of your own story," she said. "A companion to mine."

"What will we fight? Monsters? Supervillains? Dragons? Moose?"

The sky slowly turned pink in front of us, sunlight bleeding into the blue. Kyra stared at the rising dawn, and the wind played with her hair. "Fear," she said, eventually. "We'll fight fear itself."

"How?"

"By embracing it. We must not deny our fear. We have to remember to be afraid. And we have to go on anyway."

"I don't understand," I said.

"I know."

She walked to the edge of the strip and perched on a small rock. When she folded in on herself like that, she was all knees and elbows and so much smaller than I knew her to be. "I forget to be afraid sometimes. Brief moments, usually during my manic periods. I forget what it's like to be different, and I forget to be afraid."

"Don't you want to forget?" I asked.

"No." She shook her head. "I don't want to be afraid. But I do want to remember myself, who I am."

"What are you afraid of?"

"Being stuck here," she said, her voice flat. "I've told you that before."

I waited.

"Me," she continued. "I'm afraid I'll hurt myself—or

others. I'm afraid I'll hurt you." She paused. "And you," she said. "I'm terrified to lose you."

"You won't," I whispered.

"You can't promise that."

"No, I can't."

She hugged her knees to her chest. "But most of all, I'm afraid of them. Lost has a code, Cor, and I don't belong to it. I don't fit in, and they'd rather push me out. I'm a threat to them, so I can't stop being afraid, because I know they're a threat to me."

I sat down next to her on the still-frozen grass and let her lean against me. The pink sky burned into orange as the first rays of the sun touched the horizon. It lit the white-capped mountains and, inch by inch, the world around us. I'd always preferred the planets and the stars, but there was something to be said for watching the world wake up. It was a quiet wonder.

"We call them hero days," Kyra said, "because that is when we fight fear itself. And we win."

HOMEWARD BOUND

Roshan takes me to Aaron's cabin, where we spend the night. I might have managed to sleep; I'm not sure. But Roshan and Aaron stay with me, and at some point, Sam joins us too. Maybe that's all that matters. Mr. Henderson has the letter he came for, and more. Lost still has its lore, and I am safe.

I cling to my bag in the predawn twilight, as the two of them accompany me to the airstrip. I don't have my phone. I don't have most of my clothes. But I have my passport, my memories, and a way out. Part of Kyra will always be in my heart. Part of her will never be free of Lost. She will live on in the histories they tell, the stories they whisper, and the images she left behind.

When the plane touches down, Roshan walks me to it, and I have to ask, "Will you tell Kyra's story? Will you tell what happened last night?"

Roshan helps me in next to the pilot. He hands me my bag with a sad smile. And I know that, apart from the pieces I take with me, Kyra's story will never make it out of the borders of Lost. It'll grow into the legend she never wanted.

"No one would believe me any more than they would believe you. I'm sorry. But even though we failed Kyra, maybe we can honor her by living. And loving. And learning."

And maybe, I add silently, *by not keeping secrets anymore*. "Different rules. A different world."

"We can build our future, Corey. We owe it to her. I do."

I look toward the horizon, and Aaron lifts his hand from his pocket to wave. Sam stands next to him by the road.

"I told you, when we talked about the mine, Father wants to do this right if he can. So do I."

I look beyond him, toward Lost, and I know it's the last time I will see this place I once called home.

"Go to Sam, Roshan. Go home." *I'm going home too.*

Roshan steps back, and the plane's small motor makes

a mighty noise. A few minutes later, the captain begins our taxi down the runway. The pine trees on either side of the small plane blur as we pick up speed.

I lock my eyes on the deep blue sky in front of us, and I don't look back.

ALL THE LIVES WE SHARED

MY KYRA WAS NOT EXTRAORDINARY. NO MORE THAN ANY of us are—and no less either. She loved toffee and berries. She hated pears and white chocolate. Her favorite color was magenta. She loved rainstorms and snow angels and sitting in the sun with a book about anthropology or literary structure. She was a geek. She was determined. She had long nights and hero days, and she was still a girl, my girl. She was bipolar, and that was not the least of her or the best of her, but it was irrevocably part of her. She was a storyteller. And for all of her visions, she was not a visionary the way Lost wanted her to be. She was not a prophet.

Or at least, I don't remember her like that.

Instead, I choose to remember her as she was, standing at the airstrip, while Mom and Luke and I were saying our final goodbyes to Lost. She wore a gray T-shirt with pink flowers, and her long hair was tied back in a braid. Her glasses reflected the bright sun.

As we were getting ready to board the plane, she took me aside. "This'll be a new story," she said. "And it's yours to tell. But please don't leave me out of it, okay?"

I shook my head fervently. "I wouldn't. I would never."

"We'll write. You'll come visit. And then maybe next year, I can come visit you. I want to see the University of Winnipeg's Anthropology Museum, in any case. And maybe you can take me to the Royal Astronomical Society."

She knew me so well. It figured that she'd researched my new hometown better than I had. I'd been reluctant to, because doing so would make our move more real. But there on the airstrip, unable to deny the imminent change, it felt as if someone had opened a door, and now that I stood in front of it, all I wanted to do was see what was on the other side.

"I'll bring you the world," I said.

She smiled. And I didn't know—I never knew—if she was being genuine or if she was faking it to be brave.

"We'll see each other soon," I promised.

"I hope so," she said.

She was the last one standing on the airstrip as we took

off. I watched her until she was nothing more than a spot amid the green.

That is how I will remember her. And with every corner I turn, I will still expect to see her. With every constellation I observe, I'll wonder about stories as well as science. I'll build a bridge to her. I'll look for falling stars.

My regrets are not forgiveness. Neither is my dawning understanding. Not yet. Maybe not ever.

This isn't happily ever after.

But it's hope. And this is where I start a new story.

Once upon a time…

AUTHOR'S NOTE

LOST IS AN ODD PLACE, BUT KYRA'S STRUGGLES AND THE abuse she suffers are all too real. If you or someone you know struggles with mental health crises, you deserve to be supported, and you deserve to have access to the help you need. If you're thinking about suicide, you deserve immediate support. Please know there are people out there who want to provide that help.

If you're inside the United States, and you have questions about mental health and treatment options, you can reach out to:

- National Alliance on Mental Illness (NAMI) helpline: 1-800-950-NAMI (6264)

- Substance Abuse and Mental Health Services Administration (SAMHSA) national helpline: 1-800-662-HELP (4357)

If you're experiencing suicidal thoughts, please reach out to:

- National Suicide Prevention Lifeline: 1-800-273-TALK (8255)
- Trevor Project Lifeline for LGBTQ youth: 1-866-488-7386
- Crisis Text Line: text "home" to 741741

If you're a teen who prefers to talk with another teen, you can also reach out to Teen Line by calling 1-310-855-HOPE (4673). Trans Lifeline offers crisis support for trans people by trans people at 1-877-565-8860 in the United States and 1-877-330-6366 in Canada.

Helplines are available in many places and in many forms. If you're outside of the United States, you can find suicide prevention hotlines for your country via www.suicide.org/international-suicide-hotlines as well as via www.yourlifecounts.org/need-help/crisis-lines.

In Canada, crisis centers are organized by province. You can find a list of resources through the Canadian Association for Suicide Prevention (suicideprevention.ca), while MindYourMind offers both resources and interactive tools (mindyourmind.ca).

In the UK and Ireland, you can reach out to the Samaritans helpline at 116 123. In the UK, Mind provides advice and support too, via mind.org.uk and via the Mind Infoline at 0300 123 3393.

In Australia, BeyondBlue offers support and advice via beyondblue.org.au and at 1300 22 4636. Lifeline offers crisis support and suicide prevention at 13 11 14. In New Zealand, you can also reach out to Lifeline, by calling 0800 LIFELINE (543 354). If you're dealing with suicidal thoughts, call 0508 TAUTOKO (828 865). New Zealand's national mental health and addictions helpline number is 1737.

Please reach out to someone. Please know that you matter. Please stay.

ACKNOWLEDGMENTS

One of the greatest joys and greatest honors of being an author is being part of a larger community. Thank you to the many writers and creators who amaze and inspire me. To the advocates who work tirelessly to make books more welcoming and more inclusive. To the countless readers who read and shared my books, who reached out to me, who trusted with me their hopes and dreams. To you, holding this book. *Thank you*. Here's to many more.

Never-ending gratitude —

To Jennifer Udden, best and fiercest of agents. Thank you for being such a passionate champion of my stories. I'm so grateful you have my back. To Barry Goldblatt, for making me feel so at home in the BG Literary family. And to Tricia Ready, for appreciating snow as much as I do.

To Annette Pollert-Morgan, my magnificent editor. Your comments push me beyond what I thought my limits were, and your insight makes me a better author at every step of the way.

To everyone at Sourcebooks, for being such a welcoming home for me and my books: Dominique Raccah, Barb Briel, Todd Stocke, Steve Geck, Sarah Kasman, Cassie Gutman, Bret Kehoe, Michelle Lecuyer, Lynne Hartzer, Nicole Hower, Kelly Lawler, Sarah Cardillo, Danielle McNaughton, Heather Moore, Valerie Pierce, Beth Oleniczak, Alex Yeadon, Chris Bauerle, Heidi Weiland, Sean Murray, Bill Preston, Margaret Coffee, Shane White, Sara Hartman-Seeskin, Caitlin Lawler, Jennifer Sterkowitz, John Donnelly, Tina Wilson, Christy Droege, Susan Busch. You are all extraordinary. You make dreams come true.

To my foreign publishers, for letting my stories travel the world. It's such an honor.

To the stars in my night sky: Hannah Weyh, my favorite unicorn, who was the very first person I told about Corey and Kyra (back when they still had different names). Dahlia Adler, who believes in me even when I don't and whose fierce embrace of Lost Creek kept me going. Corinne Duyvis, my partner in adventures and accidental twin in all ways that count. And Fox Benwell, without whom this book would not exist and without whom I would be less than I am.

To Katherine Locke, for chats about plots, politics, publishing, and for always being there. Jessica Spotswood, for long emails and companionship. Francesca Zappia, for geeking out, terrible ideas, and awkward tapestries. Rebecca Coffindaffer, PitchMadness team cohost and community cheerleader extraordinaire. And to so many others. (You know who you are.) Thank you.

Unending gratitude to the sensitivity readers who shared their experiences with me, who read this book at various stages in the process and tirelessly helped me to shape this story and these characters: Ami Allen-Vath, Tawney Bland, Rae Chang, Ronni Davis, Lex Leonov, Tara Sim, Kayla Whaley, and those of you who wish not to be named. I am so grateful for your friendship and your generosity. What I did right was because of you; any mistakes I made are squarely on me.

To Becky Albertalli and Heidi Heilig, who fended my questions with patience and grace. You are two of the kindest, most generous people I know, and it's an honor to call you friends.

I wrote a good chunk of this book in a Scottish mansion, in amazing company. So this one goes out to the Writing Weasels. For playing Sardines in haunted hallways, exploring castles with secret libraries, and foraging our own food in the woods.

Stories lie at the heart of *Before I Let Go*, and stories have always been the heart of me too. Storytelling shaped me and saved me. Books inspire me. And in the process of working on this book, I tripped and fell into the internet and rediscovered my love for shared story worlds. Thank you to the cast, crew, and community of *Critical Role*, for being instrumental in that, for bolstering my creativity at a time when I didn't think anything could. To the parties I've played with and the players I had the honor of GMing. And especially to my YA&D crew. You're the finest, most dysfunctional party any DM could wish for. Thank you for diving headlong into a world that only exists in my imagination and for giving it life. (PS: Mind the Trickster. Watch the Thief. Beware the Dragon.)

Finally, always, to my mom, my sisters, my nephew, my closest friends, the people who know me better than I do: you are the brightest constellations. Thank you. Endlessly.

ABOUT THE AUTHOR

Marieke Nijkamp is a storyteller, dreamer, globe-trotter, geek. She holds degrees in philosophy, history, and medieval studies, has served as an executive member of We Need Diverse Books, is the founder of DiversifYA, and is a founding contributor to YA Misfits. She lives in the Netherlands. Visit her at mariekenijkamp.com.